1

Of Marriages and Music

CW01499046

Naples 1590

Few people liked to look him in the eye. I learned this from listening to what his servants said - and to what they did not say. Carlo Gesualdo, the Prince of Venosa, whenever he came to my lady's chamber I hid behind a pillar or kept my eyes cast down. Of course, he seldom noticed me.

He had a strange appearance. His face was long and narrow with a high forehead, as if it had been stretched. His lips were small and often wore a thin, cruel smile. It was the face of a zealot. He could have been a monk – or a criminal. The most extraordinary thing about him was his hands with their long fingers, like a spider. They were a musician's fingers, it was said.

His valet Bardotti laughed and said, 'a musician's fingers – or a strangler's.' He was in a position to know. Years later, an artist friend of mine would describe the look on that long face as one of frozen passion.

I can hear my lady's words in my head. 'Sort my jewels,

Laura.' How many times did I hear those words in the days leading up to her third wedding? Diamonds from the King of Spain and emeralds from the Viceroy ran through my fingers constantly, sorted, re-arranged and changed again as she paraded around the chamber trying on the vast wardrobe deemed suitable for her new status. What else could she do?

'Not yellow, my lady, trust me.' The other maid, Silvia Albano, announced this confidently as if she had come straight from the Viceroy's court or attended on the Queen of Spain. She gave me a look that could have curdled milk. 'Laura knows nothing of these things. She is just a country girl.' She meant to say, 'just a coarse peasant,' but her courage failed. As if I didn't know she came from the worst part of Palermo and her mother had been a whore.

'Yellow is very fashionable.' I muttered, 'with black lace cuffs.' Lowering my voice further I added, 'bitch!' Silvia heard me and began to screech. 'You should not keep her, my lady; she is funny in the head. She will never be any use to you.'

My lady laughed and waved her aside. She kept me with her always, as if I was some kind of lucky charm, and I have kept her always with me, in my mind and in my heart – and much good it has done for me.

'I will wear cloth of gold over white silk trimmed with silver lace for my wedding. It will be a splendid affair; something for a king's daughter.' Donna Maria's voice was flat and emotionless as she fingered the material that would be used, the silk gauze petticoats shot with gold. Her face wore the closed in look I had come to know; the voice she used when talking about the marriages that had been arranged for her.

'My Vittoria cannot join us,' she whispered. 'The prince has forbidden it. She will remain with my parents.' I kicked the folds of fabric aside with a little secret movement. All the cloth of gold in the world would not compensate for that. New husbands did not want reminders of past relationships.

My lady took refuge in the things that were available – clothes, jewels, dancing. Perhaps she thought this third marriage would be as short-lived as the others. How many times could you be married, I wondered? Surely, after this third one she would be forced into a convent. Then what would become of me? I came back to earth as Donna Maria gave me a light slap on the hand.

'Eels in spiced tomato sauce…' she gave a mirthless laugh. 'They will be served at the wedding banquet because they are the prince's favourite.'

'You hate eels,' I said; 'they give you heartburn.' She shrugged; 'Many things can give heartburn. Bring me my shawl, Laura.'

At least my mistress had been spared one of the many customs common in Naples. Widows there were obliged to cut off their hair and throw the locks onto their husband's bier. They could not marry again until their hair had grown to waist length. That was probably a Spanish commandment – they had many strange ones. I suppose Donna Maria escaped that torment because she came from Sicily.

I could not have eaten half the dishes that were served at the wedding feast, although I was always hungry. One hundred and twenty courses were offered – stuffed quails, veal steaks, goats roasted on spits, as well as the prince's eels and other fish. The servants watched from various hiding places in the gallery. Huge blocks of ice and fountains of water kept the desserts cool. I had never seen such things before.

'Carlo Gesualdo is as rich as a king,' Silvia Albano whispered.

The prince's music was played between courses. His group of musicians was his pride and joy. It was the first time I had heard those extraordinary sounds and they would ring in my head for the rest of my life, like nails being dragged over slate with a chorus of angry wasps in the background. The lack of harmony, the swooping high notes and the discordant lows made my head ache.

It was all very different from the folk tunes of my native Sicily or the melodic love songs of the Neapolitan peasants. The nobility applauded politely but many appeared bored or puzzled by the sounds. My lady nodded and smiled but I sensed she shared their feelings.

The wedding took place in the great church of the Dominicans. I was not permitted to watch but I would grow to know that place well. I often wished that the miraculous crucifix there would speak to me as it had once spoken to St. Thomas Aquinas, but I was an unworthy sinner.

Donna Maria was soon pregnant, anxious to give her husband the heir he required. I waited on her devotedly during the pregnancy, running to and fro to the convent of the Poor Clares for the sweetmeats she craved. When Don

Emanuele was born we all sighed with relief. He was a healthy, handsome baby. After the birth, the prince largely lost interest in his wife. This appeared to suit both of them very well.

We spent our time mainly in the Palace of San Severo in Naples, leased by the prince from another nobleman. My lady had visited the castle in the village of Gesualdo but she found it small and somewhat primitive – not enough marble and gilt…too many ironwork staircases. Life in the countryside bored her.

The castle was perched on a peak overlooking the small community of Gesualdo in the Southern Appenines. It dated from Norman times and the prince claimed descent from Roger 1st the Norman ruler who had conquered Sicily and southern Italy. My lady told me this, but her husband's proud lineage did not compensate her for the simplicity of her surroundings and the castle's isolation.

'There is nothing here for anyone other than peasant farmers,' she declared, looking out over the green, undulating hills. She had been accustomed to great luxury in the palaces of Palermo during her previous marriages. Her new husband owned a palace in Venosa but spent little time there. 'That place is fit only for wine making.' She longed for revelry and the liveliness of the city, and in this one thing she had her way.

Donna Maria attended as many balls and social events as she could manage, sometimes accompanied by her husband - or more often by a suitable escort. Supper parties took place on boats in the beautiful Bay of Naples. I have seen little of the world but surely there cannot be a lovelier spot on this earth.

'On the island of Capri there is an azure grotto that could have been designed by the gods for their pleasure,' Donna Maria told me when she returned one day. The prince had not been there and the music had been very agreeable. She gave me the ghost of a smile as she said this.

As for the prince, he continued to indulge his own pleasures. He loved to hunt with the Viceroy. It was considered a great honour among the Italian nobles. He was passionate about the chase, as was the aristocracy in general, Spanish as well as Italian. They loved to kill anything that moved. My lady also occasionally enjoyed the passions stirred up by the hunt. She watched on horseback with the other women, her eyes glistening as wild pigs were torn apart and boars roasted in the forest.

I often watched as they left for the hunting grounds with the Viceroy; the Prince Carlo Gesualdo, wearing his favourite velvet jacket with the pearl buttons, his perfumed gloves and golden spurs – a gift from the that same Viceroy. What a sight they were; my lady in her azure blue velvet habit, the Viceroy and his entourage, the horses, the pages, the dwarf Carnero on a white mule…the shouting, jingling and calling.

They clattered across the courtyard through the grand archway with the dogs running behind; spaniels to retrieve partridges, hounds for hare coursing, others for stag hunting. I often said a prayer to St. Eustace to protect the beautiful, gentle horses and the helpless wild things in the forest.

The Gesualdo family had done well under Spanish rule. Titles and wealth had come their way. It did no harm to their standing that they were related to many cardinals. The Spanish were so priest-ridden that they placed great score by these things. Perhaps that was why the Viceroy treated the prince leniently after the murder – or perhaps because killing your wife was not considered so terrible a crime.

2

Sicily in Darkness and Light

My lady possessed a rare and wonderful thing, a small hand glass in which you could see your face. It had been a gift from the Doge of Venice on her first marriage. Only the Venetians knew the secret of glass making and it was jealously guarded. So, for the first time one afternoon when my lady was absent I saw my reflection and realized that I was no beauty. I had the Sicilian black eyes, beaky nose and full lips. In addition, there was a black dot under my left eye that my lady said was called a mole.

Disappointed, I replaced the mirror on the chest. I already knew that my hair was a mass of unruly curls and I tried to hold them in a black velvet net. We were still living in Noto in those days, lovely Noto.

Bread and peaches and the piercing fragrance of citrus groves; these are the things I remember when I think of Noto. Most people would describe the beautiful architecture, the exquisite churches, the small but perfect city and its colourful court, but I recall the things of the senses.

Food was always scarce in the miserable Sicilian village

where I was born. Neither bread nor peaches made much of an appearance in the hovel we called home. Perhaps that is why the memory of food and certain smells has always stayed with me. I lived with my father, my three brothers and my pet goat, Tonina. Of all of them I cared only for Tonina, and she was the only one who showed me any affection.

I shall never see Noto again: it has been many years, a whole lifetime, since I spent a spring in that golden city on the southern tip of the island, but I have only to close my eyes to see purple bougainvillea and pink oleanders outside my window and the orchards of apricot, almonds and citrus in the distance

In Noto when the sun was setting the golden stones turned pink, peach, yellow and grey. Wherever you turned in the steep streets and alleyways you would see sharply sloping roofs with curling tiles, delicate domes and spires, statues of gods and goddesses flying from their plinths, a whole city floating above the fiery clouds.

I had never seen the sea until I came to the little city and I used to walk to the blue waters of the gulf whenever I could. The priest at home told us that Sicily was an island but I had never left the village.

When my lady rescued me on the highway - a wild thing, exhausted and befuddled, dark as an Arab and cross-eyed with fright, her first husband, the Marchese di San Lucido, asked 'Is she a Christian or a Moor?'

'It will be an act of charity to take her in, my lord.' Donna Maria's voice was honeyed and wheedling…'especially on this feast day of San Corrado. She will be transformed by soap and water.' I discovered that this young woman was only a year or two older than I, but she was already a wife and mother. And so, I came into my new life.

As a servant, I was always busy in the palace. My lady needed me for something constantly, to fetch this or carry that, to count her pearls or fetch her sherbert. Great ladies drank sherbert all day long while they complained to each other about the shortcomings of the servants and the problems with their lord and master.

I knew nothing of the duties of a lady's maid and so I was put in the care of a woman called Caterina who was old and slow but a terrifying disciplinarian. She had been a maid to my lady's mother and she came out of retirement to instruct me in my duties.

I practiced with a dummy and whenever I was clumsy in arranging its hair or made a mistake in laying out its clothes, Caterina would shriek and beat me with a small whip kept hidden under her skirts, I learned quickly. Until then my only skill had been in milking goats and growing vegetables. I proved to have a deft pair of hands and I was soon ready to attend Donna Maria in her chamber.

I was never a good person: my father said I was cursed because my mother died giving birth to me. He hated me for that and my brothers agreed with him.

'Because of you we lost our mother,' they would moan after father had beaten them and I had made a gruel for our supper that was inedible. The priest told me that sin came into the world through a woman and that we were not made in the image of God.

My vow to serve Donna Maria was made to a pagan, a Greek goddess, so no doubt I brought down the wrath of heaven on myself and I shall pay in the next world. The goddess was called Demeter and I found her sanctuary when I went walking one day on the edge of the city. Beyond the groves of pine and palm trees and the dim green and brown tunnels of fig trees I found a place where dozens of small, terracotta statues of women lay scattered around.

The ruined sanctuary must have been built by the Greeks who once ruled this island. My lady told me that. I knew I shouldn't pray to this goddess for fear of eternal damnation, but I loved the expressions on the faces of those tiny figures. Some were calm and impassive, others joyful, but always full of life.

That woman, the goddess, must have known how real women thought and felt because her followers looked so natural – unlike the statues of the Madonna and the saints in church that showed only religious ecstasy.

And so, it was there that I made the vow soon after I arrived in Noto, in gratitude to Donna Maria who had saved me and taken me into her service. I made it with joy and passion, little knowing where it would lead. As I knelt on the scattered stones of the shrine I looked out at the Sicilian countryside beyond, empty and sinister as it now appeared.

'I swear to serve her all my days. I will serve her until death and cherish her memory after her death, if I am able.' My voice sounded very loud in that quiet place, although I spoke in my normal voice. 'I will right any wrong done to her,' I continued bravely, as if a young peasant girl could act as a knight or even a plain soldier, but women have their ways. 'Hear me, O Lady,' I called. Then, suddenly, petrified by my daring I mumbled, 'San Corrado, hear my prayer,' as if that would make everything acceptable to heaven.

I tried not to think of the past and what had happened, telling myself never to return to the countryside but always to live in cities surrounded by high walls with streets full of people. Sometimes in the night I would wake, shuddering, seeing that lonely limestone horizon dotted with the twisted trunks of olive trees so old that those Greeks must have planted them. I saw the body of a young girl lying in a ditch fringed with yellowing grass and scarlet poppies. I knew the body belonged to me but it seemed to be in another world.

My visits to the sanctuary were, first of all, to see the wise woman, Draga Gollestani. Donna Maria had sent me there because she knew my story. I think she kept my confidence, although the other servants may have suspected the worst of me. Draga came out of her cave and stood watching me as I examined the little figurines lying on the ground. I wondered uneasily if she had heard my vow.

'The Greeks once ruled this place,' she said quietly. 'It was long ago, before the Arabs came, and the Normans. Only the Siculi were here then, the real people of this island.' She peered into my face. 'I can see you are one of them. Come inside.'

After I had swallowed the vile tasting liquid she prepared for me I wandered over to the little statues again. Draga watched me. 'Take care, my girl, those old gods had strange powers. If you pray to them your soul will be damned forever. That's what the priests will tell you!' She gave a loud snort and went back into the cave. I walked back to the palace. So, she had heard my vow, but I knew she would not care.

I never saw Draga or the sanctuary again after that day. Whether it was due to her foul medicine or my prayers to San Corrado, the patron of Noto, I do not know, but I did not become pregnant as a result of my ordeal.

It happened soon after my father betrothed me to the son of a neighbour, a muleteer whose poverty was almost as great as our own. Enrico was ill-favoured and little better than a dwarf, but the arrangement suited my father who wanted only one less mouth to feed, especially mine. I was thirteen and I would take as my dowry one chemise, a cooking pot and three Spanish coins that had belonged to my mother. I knew nothing of life outside the village; I only knew that I did not want to marry Enrico. I wept in secret for the mother I had never known believing that her presence might have saved me from my fate.

Just before the wedding was due to take place the peddler came to the village. His name was Guido Lotti and his arrival was always a great occasion for the women and girls. I heard his triumphal procession along the dirt track between the houses. When he came to where I was tending little Tonina he stopped and looked down at me. His eyes were black and opaque. Looking into them like looking into the darkness of a deep well shaft. Years later I would meet another man with eyes like that and I would know at once that he was evil.

'I hear you're to be married, little Laura,' he said. 'You have grown up at last.' His eyes flickered over me as I held out a coin my brother Leonardo had given me.

'I want to buy a ribbon to wear on my wedding day.' He laughed because I had never had money to buy his wares before.

'You don't seem very happy, little Laura. I thought all young girls wished to be married.'

'I do not care for Enrico!' I muttered. He laughed again and held up a fistful of coloured ribbons. He pointed towards the scorched brown hillside, pock marked with cactus plants.

'Walk a little way with me, Laura. You can tell me all your troubles. Choose the finest ribbon. It will be my wedding gift to you.' He walked away not looking to see whether I followed or not. The devil's gifts must be paid for with blood and tears and your very soul. If only I had known that.

Of course, I followed him like an obedient puppy, as I would have followed anyone who showed an interest in me – also, the promise of a free gift was irresistible. My father would be furious but hopefully he would never know. It was two o'clock and the barren hills shimmered in the furnace of the sun. I brushed my damp hair away from my face and caught up with the peddler. Without looking at me he grasped my hand and pulled me along.

'Have you ever been to Noto, little Laura?' he asked, knowing very well that I had never left the village. 'It's full of great golden palaces and churches. The nobles wear the finest silks and velvets and walk among the orange groves. We can be there in two days. Will you come with me?'

'My…my father would never allow it,' I stammered. 'I'm betrothed; I should never have come this far. Let me have the ribbon and I'll go back.'

He laughed – he was always laughing – but there was no merriment in his laughter. We passed sparse groves of olive trees, twisted like old men, and came to a group of strangely shaped stones taller than our cottage. In the distance, I could see the faint white glimmer of a road winding through the low hills.

The peddler threw his tray to the ground, spread out his cloak, and stretched himself upon it, chin in hand. 'Make your choice, little Laura.' I knelt down and examined the coloured bundles self-consciously, aware of his blank eyes boring into my back. When I felt his hands caress my neck, pushing away the shawl and wandering over my body, I went rigid with fear.

'Don't be afraid, little Laura,' he whispered as I continued to kneel with the ribbons clenched in both hands. Suddenly, I dropped the ribbons and tried to scramble away from him, but he gripped me viciously and pulled me onto the cloak. He was slight of build but very strong. As he tore at my clothes he whispered in my ear. 'I saw it in the cards this morning, Laura. You were meant to be mine. The cards never lie.'

As he fondled my nakedness I felt my flesh creep with horror. I was a country girl, reared among animals, and I knew where these things led. I also knew that my father would kill me and, according to the priest, my soul would roast in hell for all eternity.

I was too terrified to cry out but I struggled to the end until he overpowered me. The sharp, animal smell of his body pressed against mine has remained with me all my life.

When, at last, it was over and I lay torn and bleeding on the ground, the peddler ignored my sobs and began to repack his tray neatly. He swung his cloak with a carefree gesture and prepared to leave. Only then did he look down at me and say, 'you can join me in Noto if you like, little Laura, only two days from here!' He threw a few ribbons over my shaking body before he left.

I do not remember how long I lay there sobbing, but pain and thirst forced me to get up. I tried to re-arrange my torn dress. I tied up the mess of my hair and staggered blindly towards the road. Somewhere in my mind I wondered why no-one had come to find me, and what would happen if I returned to the village, but I already knew the answer.

Hours must have passed by the time I stumbled onto the road. For a few moments, I was enveloped in total darkness as I lay in a ditch. Then the moon rose and hovered over me. I was crazed with thirst and I could not remember my prayers. I scarcely remembered who I was or where I had come from. Holy Mother help me!

As I lay in the ditch, watching that unforgiving white light I heard the faint sound of bells in the distance, then the beat of horses' hooves and the jingling of harness. I knew I would have only one chance. Gathering all my strength I crawled into the middle of the road and waited for death.

Strange, is it not, that a single small gesture can change a life? I should have been trampled to death by the horses. They were close enough for me to feel the steam from their nostrils and the shaking of the ground from their hooves, but I was spared. I was saved by the skill of a coachman who could stop his animals even on the brink of a precipice by a light touch on the reins.

Inside the coach sat my saviour and my nemesis, Donna Maria d'Avalos, and her disapproving companion – disapproving of me, naturally, and Donna Maria's decision to take me with her. She wiped my face with a silk cloth and gave me sips of water and wine. 'We will take her with us,' she told her companion. 'She has been set upon by brigands, no doubt.'

To this day I don't know why she took pity on me, a tattered, wild thing, but she was not a typical aristocrat. Mostly, we're invisible to them…not quite human. That is how I came into her service.

3

Noto to Naples

When I look back at that time in Noto it remains the happiest period of my life. Although I had nothing of my own and I was at the beck and call of my betters, I had no real responsibilities. I had been released from the horrors of my early life and I had no idea of the person I would become, what I would see and the things I would be driven to do. If we could see into the future what would we do? In Sicily they would say, "So be it." There is nothing to be done and death comes soon enough.

I tiptoed out of the chamber and went to the kitchens to fetch a goblet of sherbert. My lady would be thirsty when she woke. The summer heat was fierce yet the cook was busy making sugar fancies. Boiling vats of sugar filled the room with unbearable sweet heat and a perspiring kitchen boy was dabbing ice water on the cook's forehead whenever she seemed about to faint.

I loved being in the kitchen despite the heat. Gossip and slander flew back and forth with roars of laughter from the unruly staff. My people are great liars, vengeful and passionate.

Reputations can be destroyed in a moment and enemies or friends made for life. I remember a saying I heard in my village, "blood washes blood."

I had good friends among the servants and the cook was fond of me, a poor orphan who had been rescued from near death, as she told everyone. It was she who told me that my lady's husband, the Marchese, was unwell. He was often sick and the men joked that he was exhausted by the demands of a young wife, but the cook knew better. She took a certain amount of enjoyment in predicting misfortune for her betters.

'He has the sweating sickness,' she declared. 'He will never be truly well.'

It was a worrying thought because Donna Maria had recently given birth and needed to avoid any malady.

'Perhaps we will go to Palermo now,' I said. The cook laughed and slapped the boy who had slackened his cooling duties. 'Palermo would be even worse; people are dying from heat and disease there. My cooking will restore him!' The kitchen boy snickered and received another slap for his pains. I stole a sliver of cooled sugar and went in search of the sherbert.

Soon after I was told that we were bound for Naples.

Naples. The great city! I was both thrilled and terrified at the prospect of seeing it for the first time. The cook put me right.

'You will soon wish yourself back in Sicily,' she sniffed. 'It is a fearsome place; huge and full of murderous thieves and vagabonds. Palermo is bad enough, mark my words!'

She returned to the sugar fancies while I collected the clean linen. Soon we would leave to spend some time at the Viceroy's court.

We set off by ship for Messina where we would board another ship for the journey to the mainland. Nobody attempted to cross the island overland with its unmade roads and bands of brigands.

Naples was as hot and lively as hell, according to the other servants who knew it well. I had never seen such narrow streets and tall houses, such huge palaces and churches and vast crowds of people. I had not thought there were so many people in the world. Donna Maria said it was the largest city in Europe, but I did not know where Europe was.

Often, I was afraid to go among the throngs in the streets unless someone accompanied me. I feared I would be swallowed up and never seen again.

'You are a strange creature,' Donna Maria laughed. 'You are full of fancies.' I had told her about being swallowed up. It may have been a fancy to her but she never needed to push her way through the crowds where gleaming palaces stood next to rows of hovels. She travelled everywhere in a litter. Her main pre-occupation at this time was the new wardrobe she had acquired for the visit.

Her questions were endless; 'Is the gown too tightly corseted? Should the sleeves be narrow or slashed? How high should the lace ruff stand?' I patiently offered my opinion. My eye was good and I understood colour, although I knew little of the latest Spanish fashions.

My lady had been well received at court. The Spanish were entranced by her blonde curls and blue eyes; "The fairest of the fair" they called her. It was there that she met the Prince Carlo Gesualdo for the first time. He was her cousin, but it seemed to me that all the nobility were related to each other. This prince composed music which he played in public at every opportunity. The cousins paid little attention to each other but their meeting would have grave consequences for us all. I remember only his long face and long fingers.

Then the Marchese began to sicken again and we returned to Sicily. By the time we reached Messina he was dying. He was too sick to carry on to his home and so we remained in Messina lodging in a convent where the nuns ministered to him. His valet said the Marchese had eaten melons before he left Naples, a fruit notorious for causing sickness. We heard him groaning and smelled the stink from his chamber as the servants ran around changing the sheets and strewing herbs.

'He died of a putrid fever and flux,' announced the cook who always knew everything. And so, Donna Maria arrived home as a widow and almost two years were to pass before we saw Naples again.

Fevers and pestilence were sweeping the island and the baby, Don Ferrante, died only weeks after his father. Donna Maria's parents appeared looking like black-robed angels of doom. Within a few weeks of the funeral they arranged a second marriage for their daughter to another nobleman, the Marchese di San Guilianova. Donna Maria walked around in a daze. She had scarcely met her husband-to-be for more than a half hour when she entered the church for the wedding. We went to live in a different palace with different servants but as always, my mistress took me with her.

The Marchese's family had lands and titles in the Abruzzo region but he also had a palace in Palermo near the Termini gate. It was beautifully appointed with a gilded ballroom decorated with a frescoed ceiling depicting Daphnis and Chloe. I loved to gaze up at those nymphs and gods, their beautiful bodies half unclothed, surrounded by the fruits of paradise.

This second husband was as proud and arrogant as any Sicilian nobleman. Once when his carriage became stuck against another nobleman's carriage in a narrow street, neither would give way for fear of losing face. They stayed in that position for hours before continuing on horseback. The servants enjoyed that story for many days.

We were not often in Palermo, but I always enjoyed our time there. Donna Maria made many visits to friends and relatives in the city and that gave me more free time than usual. I loved to wander around the Vucciria market which had been on the same spot since the Arabs ruled this island. We ate and drank better in Palermo than in any other place. Sicilian food is superior to anything found on the mainland. Dio mio! The spices, the delicacy of the ingredients – wonderful.

By making friends with the stall holders I was able to get tastings of all my favourites, arancini, stuffed fried rice balls and maccu, creamy fava bean soup flavoured with wild fennel. Anything flavoured with fennel was heavenly for me. I would wander around eating chick pea fritters flavoured with lemon, taking in the colour and the cries, the brightly decorated little carts trundling by.

Sometimes I would call at the convents, especially La Martorana, which was famous for its almond paste fancies. Donna Maria loved them and I was able to secrete one or two for myself. The finest treat of all was cassata but it seldom came my way.

Palermo was not a large city but it was full of splendid buildings. It was not as beautiful, as perfect as Noto but it was full of life. I remember the huge fountain in Piazza Pretoria that was called the "fountain of shame" because it featured statues of nude women. There was the great royal palace and, most wonderful of all to a country girl, there was the church of La Martorana full of exquisite mosaics made by craftsmen from Constantinople.

Donna Maria often went to mass there and I would accompany her. Her main interest there was one of the young priests but on that occasion she was content simply to observe. I frequently forgot my prayers because I was staring open mouthed at the mosaics. I had never seen anything so lovely, not even in Noto.

Gazing at the mosaics, I felt transported back in time. Donna Maria was right; there were layers and layers of history on this island. Lost in admiration I continued to gaze until my mistress tugged impatiently at my arm. We were ready to leave.

I loved and hated my homeland with a passion. Those

years in Sicily were a kind of lull before the main drama of my life.

I believe that my attachment to Donna Maria and her fondness for me lay in the fact that we kept each other's secrets. Of course, she knew my secret from the beginning. Had she not rescued me from the roadside after my ordeal? But I soon learned that my mistress had a hidden side to her personality. Outwardly she was the demure noblewoman, so fair and angelic in appearance, but she was also passionate and fiery, and she sought relief from her dull, unremarkable husbands with young lovers as passionate as herself.

'Are you shocked little Laura?' she asked me, laughing at my serious expression when she commanded me to carry messages to her lovers. I suppose I was shocked, but I quickly realized that the nobility lived by its own rules. Perhaps God or the Pope gave them a special dispensation. They had choices that were not available to the rest of us. We had no choices at all. At least my lady knew that I would not betray her. There was always an unspoken understanding between us. I never told her of my vow but I think she knew it instinctively.

She was careful in her choice of paramour. They were kept well away from the household gossips. Once, greatly daring, she took her confessor as a lover, a handsome young monk who conveniently left to become a missionary in the Americas after a few months of pleasuring her. In most of these adventures I aided her in many ways. I pretended to go to confession so that I could give the priest lover my lady's messages. Southerners liked to make love in the afternoon.

What did it matter? I was keeping my vow and already I felt that I had nothing to lose. Donna Maria was not a saint, but she had been my saviour.

4

Gesualdo

When my mistress wanted to talk, Silvia would be sent away and I remained in the chamber. I was not exactly her confidante – she was too grand for that, but I was her accomplice and therefore kept close. I recall the ways in which she would learn my opinion without appearing to ask for it. That would have been demeaning for her.

'What did you think of Father so and so, Laura? Did you think him handsome?' She would ask, knowing full well that I had been taking messages to him for some time. In the same way, she would prise information from me about the gossip in the city. 'What did you hear in the market, in the piazzas?' And I would tell her what I had heard about other noble lords and ladies. My information usually came from their servants. Donna Maria liked to keep abreast of everything.

Those years in Sicily flew by. In 1590 I was twenty four years old, as far as I knew. Men had tried to woo me but I refused them. Their touch made my flesh crawl. The peddler had ruined me for normal life, or so I thought. I believed my future lay with Donna Maria, while the men in the household took to calling me the nun or *la frigida* behind my back. I suppose I was content enough with my lot.

Then the second husband died. The household stunned: he had been perfectly healthy when he returned from inspecting his lands.

'He is just fatigued,' his valet told us. Then suddenly he was dead in his chamber, his face purple and contorted. Everyone suspected poison but the physician said it was his heart that had stopped. Old fool! Your heart generally did stop when you died, but if he was poisoned no-one was ever blamed and no trace of poison was found.

I sensed that a big change was on the horizon. Donna Maria wore a closed in expression as if she was trying not to be present at all. She maintained it very well until her vulture parents arrived. They were soon on the scene, grave-faced, black-clad as always, but not betraying any emotion. This time they had very special plans for their daughter. She would leave Sicily forever and return to Naples where she would wed her cousin Prince Carlo Gesualdo of Venosa, the composer. I saw the look of shock on her face after they told her the good news. What could she do? Hadn't my father planned to sell me? That is what daughters are for.

'I shall be a princess, Laura,' my lady said in a dead voice. Then she perked up a little as if she had remembered something. 'You will come with me, of course.' I nodded. 'My gowns must have a train from now on; princesses always have trains.'

That was how we said farewell to my native island. I

knew in my bones that I would never see it again. Did I care? Sicily had not cared about me, but I felt sorrow when I remembered Noto, beautiful Noto, that I had left forever.

Donna Maria did not register any strong feelings about her third marriage after the first shock. Perhaps she wept in secret but I doubt it. She probably regarded it as normal practice for her kind of people. I think the nobility are worse than the common folk in that respect; buying and selling their children for a piece of land here, a title there, currying favour with King or Pope.

We would be part of the household of Gesualdo and Donna Maria would become my black angel with the golden hair. What happened to her would force me to live my life a certain way, to become something wicked. I had to fulfill my vow to the goddess.

Carlo Gesualdo was the second son in his family and had not expected to inherit the title. His brother had died of the plague and so Don Carlo took on his role. He had not been in any hurry to marry, we heard. His passions were music and hunting. Now he needed an heir and his cousin was available.

'She'll do,' I expect he thought. 'She is fertile and widowed and my relative…perfect.'

Permission had to be obtained from the Holy Father because they were first cousins and because the official period of mourning for the second husband was not over. The vulture parents arranged everything very quickly. They came, they hovered, they struck and they departed. Indeed, the second husband was scarcely cold in his grave before we were setting off for Naples.

5

Unicorn Powder

My mistress was talking to herself in the mirror when the merchant appeared in the courtyard. She was complaining *sotto voce* about the heat, the boredom of her life and the absence of the poet, Tasso, who would have entertained her with his verses.

'Even the castle at Gesualdo would be preferable to this,' she moaned. Seeing my look of surprise, she added, 'at least it is in the hills and therefore cooler. The heat in Naples in July is intolerable.' I brought her Hungary water to dab on her neck and perfumed the chamber with bergamot and spices but it helped little.

When I looked out of the window I saw a horseman ride into the courtyard. He and his mount were covered in a fine white dust like equine ghosts. His red-rimmed eyes and the black runnels of dirt on his face gave him the appearance of a sinister carnival clown, something to give nightmares to a child. He slid from his mount in slow motion. The beast looked as exhausted as its rider. I called to my lady and she came to peer out of the window.

'That poor horse will not survive; tell the servants to attend to them. Nobody should be travelling in this heat.' She returned to the mirror again. I went out of the chamber. When I returned I told her that the horseman, a merchant, had asked for an audience.

'He claims he has a rare treasure brought from Venice. It is powdered unicorn's horn straight from a galley newly arrived from Cathay where those beautiful creatures roam free - he says!' This speech came out in a rush and the effect on my lady was astonishing. She stood in the middle of the chamber, her face aglow with pleasure and relief.

'This could be the answer to our prayers, Laura. You know that little Emanuele is sick and fevered. Powdered unicorn's horn is a powerful remedy and an antidote against the plague.'

Rumours were rife in Naples that the plague was among us, but disease was ever present in this great port city. My lady must have seen the doubt in my expression.

'What is it?' she asked, her voice sharp. 'Is something amiss?'

'I think the man could be a charlatan,' I told her. 'The powder comes in a jewelled coffret and the price is two hundred ducats.' Her face blanched but she recovered quickly.

'No matter; bring him here. I must see for myself.' I left the room feeling uneasy. In the servants' quarter men were whispering that the Venetian merchant had never been near a unicorn - or its horn. Wagers were being taken at that moment.

The merchant was sitting on a bench near the kitchen door with his legs splayed out in an attitude of total weariness. He had washed the dust from his face and hands and poured a small river of liquid down his throat. When I addressed him his eyes snapped open and he scrambled to his feet at once.

'My mistress will see you now. Follow me.' As we climbed the stairs to my lady's apartment we passed Emanuele's nursery and I heard the low, plaintive cry of a sick child.

The man bowed low before my lady. When he laid the coffret on a bed of violet velvet we could see that it was, indeed, a beautiful thing; a tiny, perfect box made of chased gold set with amethysts and pearls.

'Cellini.' said the merchant in an authorative tone. 'It is definitely the work of Benvenuto Cellini.'

'Or at least by one of his pupils,' murmured my lady.

'I assure you, your graciouseness...' My lady smiled at him and gestured at the table.

'Please take some refreshment, signore, while I examine the piece.' The man accepted eagerly and I set out almond wafers and Lagrime Christi, the sweet wine from Vesuvius. My lady attempted to open the little box unsuccessfully. 'Show me the powder.'

The merchant fumbled a little then extracted a tiny phial from the coffret. He poured a small amount of brownish white powder onto a piece of silk. I sniffed at it but I caught only a whiff of jasmine and sandalwood, the warm perfumes of the south. Did unicorns smell of jasmine, I wondered? Meanwhile, the merchant continued his patter.

'His Spanish Majesty always carries some of this powder on his person,' he assured us.

'I thought the Spanish only carried relics of the saints under their hair shirts,' my lady replied. The man smiled uneasily. We knew it was unwise to mock our overlords, but my lady was at ease in her own chamber. She beckoned to me and I brought a small chest over to the merchant.

'I will buy your amulet,' she smiled. The man looked relieved as I showed him the ducats.

Afterwards, when the merchant had taken his leave we watched from the window as the prince commanded his men to shoot into the sky repeatedly in an attempt to induce some movement of the air. Dust shimmered in the courtyard like a million tiny pieces of silver. The air was stifling and I knew that my mistress feared for her little son. His fever could signal the beginning of something worse. The prince has no fear of the plague, perhaps because that was how he gained the title and the family estates.

When my lady retired for her afternoon rest I sat outside her room with my sewing listening to her husband employing his own remedy for all ills, the music of the archlute. He was playing one of his own compositions, a madrigal called *Felice Primavera*, joyful spring, set to a poem by his favourite writer, Torquato Tasso. The subject of the prince's compositions always seemed unimportant to me. The same languishing, high pitched, tortured notes were used in everything he wrote.

My lady called to me, peevish because she could not sleep. 'Bathe my temples with lavender water,' she commanded, and when she turned away I refreshed myself in the same way.

'We should have asked the merchant to tell us tales of the Serenissima while he was here,' she lamented. Neither of us had visited Venice, but it was said that nobody should die before they had seen the water city.

That night, as I helped her to dress for dinner, the coffret was suspended from her waist on a thin golden chain. She wore a gown of embroidered amethyst silk over an underskirt of silver tissue. I took extra trouble with her hair, weaving seed pearls and violet silk among her curls. I was pleased with my efforts as she descended the stairs. Her husband watched her from the loggia below and I saw his glance noting the coffret. His lips did not move as she reached him, but little escapes his notice in this household. Although he spends hours making music, his valet Bardotti acts as his eyes and ears.

Peering from the shadows of the gallery I saw the prince's musicians gathered in the dining hall, headed by Pomponio Nenna, the director of music and Mutio Effrem, the composer. The talk was all of contrapuntal practice and double counterpoint; words that were meaningless to me and also to my lady.

From time to time the prince leaned towards his wife and said, 'Is that not so, my dear?'

She nodded and smiled and sipped her wine, her high collar of lace and pearls waving like a peacock's tail as she moved. Donna Maria was so proud of her high collars; "in the mode of Maria Stuarda," a reference to the fashion set by the unhappy Queen of Scots.

Don Gesualdo loved to play humiliating games with

people, with his family, his retainers, even with the Spanish courtiers of the Viceroy - but especially with his wife. Sometimes she took a small revenge, such as the purchase of the unicorn powder. One day she may take a larger one.

As I slipped away from the gallery I met Carnero the jester preparing to entertain the prince and princess. He was my only real friend among the servants. I had not grown close to anyone else in Gesualdo's household. Carnero always knew everything at least a day before anyone else.

'They will leave Naples soon,' he told me. 'There is an invitation from the Viceroy. Of course, the master doesn't want to leave. He would rather suffer the heat if it means he can spend all day in his music room.' He smiled and hopped away on his tiny misshapen legs, almost tripping over the steward's one-eyed cat that found its way into every nook and cranny.

After dinner, they went to see little Emanuele and I followed at a discreet distance. The child was sleeping peacefully enough but his face was flushed against the white sheet, the skin dry and hot. The nursemaid, fearful in the presence of her master, gabbled at top speed.

'The herbal medicine given by the apothecary has reduced the fever somewhat. The child ate a little and was not in any pain, my lord...my lady.' She bobbed up and down in her starched white apron. My lady frowned and tried to linger near the crib but the prince was satisfied with this report and urged everyone not to worry. He has forgotten the death of his wife's second child. How can a mother not worry about her sick infant? My lord prefers to ignore his wife's previous marriages and, naturally, the children of those marriages. Little Ferrante is in heaven and as for Vittoria, Donna Maria has not seen her these past eighteen months for fear of annoying the prince. The child remains with the vulture parents in Sicily.

If Emanuele dies I do not know how my lady would recover from such a blow. The thought was too terrible to bear. The house of Gesualdo would be without an heir and there was little likelihood of another. The prince has not sought her bed for many weeks. The gossip is that he did not wish to marry at all because he prefers boys, but it was necessary after he inherited the family title. Everyone knows that music is his real and abiding love.

As he left the nursery my mistress slipped the amulet into my hand and I placed it under the child's pillow, warning the nurse not to remove it that night. When I slipped into the corridor I saw the prince leaning against a window ledge looking out over the rooftops of Naples, now scarcely visible in the hot, purple night. Golden pinpricks of light pierced the darkness from the city beyond the gates and the cry of the watchman floated up from the piazza. I suddenly felt drained and tired and longed for my bed, although it was too hot to sleep in comfort. From the shadows, I heard my mistress bid her husband goodnight. He muttered to himself,

'Perhaps it is time to leave the city; the air is oppressive.' Turning to Donna Maria he added, 'We have an invitation to visit Chiaia. Don Garzia of Toledo is giving a house party and we cannot refuse an invitation from the Viceroy.'

Her voice betrayed no emotion. 'I will prepare for the journey tomorrow morning.' He bowed his head and his glance flickered over her He must have noticed the absence of the coffret but he said nothing. As she walked away he stared at her retreating figure as if his eyes could bore through her body. I shuddered, as I always did in his presence.

Next morning, as I helped Silvia Albano, to pack the clothes, the valet Bardotti appeared with a note from the prince. It asked for an account of my lady's expenditure for the past month - in detail. She clenched her teeth in fury and I laughed.

'Powdered unicorn's horn does not come cheap, my lady.'

She pretended to slap me and tried to smile. Donna Maria had her own money and disliked being held to account for every scudi. At least her husband would have to admit that the amulet was effective. Little Emanuele was almost his normal self that morning.

We left Naples a few days later with a sense of relief. The prince rode ahead of his entourage on his favourite grey as the horses and carriages clattered out of the courtyard into the narrow streets of the city, now deserted and evil smelling. Only the rats peered out for a fleeting moment from piles of rotting refuse. Fear of the plague had paralysed the city.

It was very early in the morning, just after first light, and we hoped to arrive at our destination before dark that day. The nobility disliked early rising and my mistress yawned and complained for an hour or two while Emanuele and his nurse dozed in a corner of the carriage.

After we had eaten a little bread and some peaches Donna Maria became more cheerful, playing with the child for a while when he woke. Then I was ordered to produce the cards from the hiding place in my basket. I knew what she meant. The cards were the Tarrochi, forbidden by the Church, but consulted by everyone in Naples. The future lay within them and those who did not possess their own consulted them through gypsy fortune-tellers.

Donna Maria consulted them often, although never when the prince was around. She had explained to me that she knew something of the meanings of the various pictures. They might indicate that a journey would be taken, a girl child would be born (a calamity), or luck at gambling. If once you understood the significance of the pictures the future could be predicted. I do not know how my mistress gained this knowledge but many things were possible in Sicily where we had both been born.

Now she pored over the cards, her blue, short-sighted eyes as close to the pictures as possible. I had looked at them often enough, but they were just pictures to me.

She laid out just three cards on her lap. 'This is the simplest spread,' she explained. The cards were the Nine of Swords, Temperance and the Sun.

Donna Maria explained that the Swords card indicated that there was a lot of anxiety in the past, 'due to bad people,' milady said. Her smile changed to a scowl for a moment. She turned up the Temperance card, 'Now things will become more harmonious and the problems will fade away.' I failed to see the truth of that as far as the prince was concerned. The Sun card indicated a lot of happiness in store, something special. Then the cards were carefully folded away.

She stared out of the window at the countryside passing slowly by with a faraway look on her face. She murmured something under her breath that I could not catch. Emanuele began to grizzle. Then she turned to me and smiled.

'I shall meet someone at Chiaia in the next few days. I shall meet my destiny; it is written in the cards.' I knew little about the cards but I had learned that it was better to have them read by another person. I suggested this to my lady but she just smiled that dreamy smile and said it did not matter.

Looking back, I can see that the journey to Chiaia marked the end of my happy time with Donna Maria. Events would be set in motion that would lead to a great tragedy. It would be my burden to carry the knowledge of those events for the rest of my life. I had been marked from my birth, cursed because I caused the death of my mother. My path through life would always be crossed with sorrow and violence. It was fortunate for me and for my lady that we knew nothing of our real destinies as we gazed at the passing countryside, smelling the tang of the sea as we came closer to our destination.

6

A Peacock Lover

Chiaia: it all began in that place - twenty aristocrats, rich as sin and with nothing to do except intrigue with each and make love with someone's spouse. Trouble was bound to happen.

The kitchens were chaotic with servants running around carrying messages, newly pressed doublets and gowns, trays of food and wine, and harassing the Viceroy's servants who tried to give orders to everyone. Someone shoved a plate of food into my hands.

'Take it while you can. There's scarcely enough for everyone.' I recognized a girl I knew from another household in Naples. We found a space and chewed on our dried meat and bread. The other girl had some fruit and water to share.

I saw the prince's valet, Bardotti, whispering in a corner with his cronies. These occasions were an opportunity to exchange the gossip of the city. The prince relied on Bardotti to keep him abreast of the scandals. As I swallowed some hard cheese and weak wine, passed to us by a page, I heard him say that his master hoped to play some of his compositions to the company that evening. There was a good deal of laughing and grimacing at that news.

One of the Viceroy's servants called out to him,

'Heh, Bardotti. Come over here!' The man rounded on him at once.

'I'm Sire Bardotti to you, boy. I answer only to Don Gesualdo.' He was getting above himself again – and in the Viceroy's own house. I wondered how long it would take for our master to realize this and do something unpleasant. It depended on how indispensable the valet was to him.

The girl I knew from Naples urged me to join her for the servants' dinner that evening.

'Don't hide away in the apartment. There will be good company, wine and dirty jokes!' She nudged me good naturedly and I promised to attend but my mood was unsettled and I did not relish a large gathering in the sweltering kitchens. I was troubled by my lady's words, "I will meet my destiny at Chiaia." The images conjured up by this announcement were destroying my appetite. I had met my destiny once and my life had been almost torn from me.

For months, I had watched Donna Maria growing more bored and dissatisfied with her life. Perhaps she was tired of being passed from husband to husband, finally reaching the Prince of Venosa, the man with the dead eyes, who loved only music and horses.

She had her own amusements: sometimes her eyes would flicker appraisingly over a handsome page in the palace service, linger over a well turned leg or broad shoulders. The demon of lust can overcome us at any time, although it seldom troubled me. Guido Lotti was responsible for that. Feeling uneasy, I returned to the chamber wondering what I could do to protect my mistress, as I felt bound to do. She had saved me and when that happens you are always in debt to your saviour.

After I dressed Donna Maria in a gown of pale blue and white silk I placed ropes of pearls around her neck and watched her as she descended the stairs with her lord. I made my way through the brilliantly lit corridors to an alcove in the musicians' gallery where I could hide and look down on the banqueting hall. Why did I do this? I could have been resting my tired bones, eating and drinking with the servants, relaxing, sharing gossip. Instead I was squashed into a dark corner watching my betters enjoying themselves on the finest food and wine available, using the most splendid gold and silver dishes. I only knew that I must look to my mistress in any way I could.

Looking down I saw a wonderful scene in the great hall. Hundreds of the finest beeswax candles blazed and perfumed vapour rose from braziers, filling the air with the scent of summer flowers. There was a throng of lords and ladies dressed in bright silks and velvets. The Viceroy himself wore a cape of cloth of gold tissue with his jewelled seal of office around his neck. Servants stirred the air with large fans of palm and feathers. Two- pronged silver forks flashed in the candlelight. Miraculously, the guests avoided stabbing themselves.

I shrank further into my corner as the musicians took their places in the gallery. I caught a glimpse of the prince asking the Viceroy for leave to go up and instruct them. He positively glowed with pride and joy at that moment. Gesualdo sought every opportunity to play for guests, however unappreciative they might be. Everything else was forgotten as the music spoke.

I looked down to find my mistress, seeing the pale dress amid a sea of dark materials. She was in profile and I could see her animated expression as she nodded and smiled at the person seated opposite. I leaned out of my corner a little to gain a better view of this figure, despite my terror of the prince catching sight of me. He would have had me whipped.

He was a young, handsome man dressed in vivid green and blue silk with a green velvet cape. His dark hair and beard and the glow of the green and blue made him seem like a peacock displaying his beauty to the world - and to one person in particular.

I felt a cold trickle of sweat at my neck as I watched them, thankful that the prince was turned away from the guests to conduct the musicians. At that moment the notes of his first madrigal began to fill the air, *Dolcissimo Sospiro* – sweetest sigh.

Donna Maria and the peacock did not seem to notice as they continued to talk animatedly. It was as if no one else existed.

'Your sweet sigh is not for me but for another,' the singers chorused plaintively. For a brief moment, his hand covered hers as he offered her a sweetmeat. I crossed myself in dread in my hiding place. By the time the musical interlude was over I was stiff and aching, scarcely able to hobble away to the apartment.

When I helped her to undress that night my mistress glowed like a church candle.

'What a wonderful evening, Laura!' she exclaimed. 'I'm so glad we came after all.'

'My lord seemed to enjoy playing his music for the company.' I commented.

'Hmmm,' she said before chattering on about the guests, the jewels and the plans for tomorrow. I do not think she recalled a single note.

'Who was the handsome man in green and blue, my lady?' I asked casually. She blushed and turned her head away. 'Oh, that was the Duke of Andria. So unfortunate that his wife could not come with him…she is visiting her parents.' We discussed what she would wear tomorrow. A picnic lunch in the garden was planned. As Donna Maria knelt to pray, her white shift billowing around her, there seemed to be more than usual passion in her silent requests.

I was kept busy in the apartment for the following three days and I saw little of my lady except for mornings and evenings. All I know was that she grew more animated as each day passed and surely her husband must have been truly blind not to have noticed. Of course, a gossiping servant noticed and happily supplied the facts as we gathered in the kitchen for the evening meal.

'Your lady and the duke haven't wasted much time, have they?' she sniggered. Several people stopped whatever they were doing to listen. Pages and scullery boys stood open mouthed with anticipation. I was thankful that Bardotti was not present.

'What do you mean?' I snapped. But I knew very well what she meant. 'I suppose you heard someone gossiping?' I said accusingly. The woman bridled.

'I didn't need to listen to gossip, my girl. I saw it with my own eyes.'

The cook drew in her breath loudly. 'What did you see? Out with it!' The woman looked around proudly, savouring her moment. 'I saw it as plain as anything, that Donna Maria d'Avalos making eyes at the Duke of Andria - couldn't keep their hands off each other, could they? I was told to bring her some smelling salts because she was feeling faint, but when I came with them she was inside one of the grottoes with the Duke.'

'And?' gasped the cook.

'Well, I didn't go in because I could tell what was going on from the noises. She didn't sound faint to me!' The pages giggled and nudged each other. I managed only a feeble retort. 'I thought you said you saw everything? You haven't any proof.' The assembled company rounded on me and called me a fool.

'They're all the same, those lords and ladies,' sniffed the cook, 'loose women- and the men are no good either.' The maid nodded, 'and those Spaniards are just as bad, if you ask me, for all their black clothes and religious ways.' The company nodded in unison and laughed at me as they went on with their work.

'You might be looking for another place when the husband finds out,' said one.

'That Prince of Venosa looks like a man who bears a grudge,' said another. If only they knew. Carnero gave me a warning look. He was sitting nearby, but for once he said nothing.

I walked away and hid in the gardens for a while hoping to disprove the gossip but knowing in my heart that it must be true. When I saw them, they were emerging from one of the small grottoes. My lady's hand caressed the sea shells adorning the arch. She was looking up at the duke and laughing, her left hand, trailing over the stones. As they moved away his hand rested lightly in the small of her back and her right hand was placed momentarily on his chest.

They moved across the garden out of my sight but that moment of intimacy revealed everything. Donna Maria was hopelessly in love, possibly for the first time in her life. I shivered, although the heat was so fierce that my gown was sticking to my back. Just as I turned to creep away I saw Don Giulio Gesualdo, the prince's uncle, emerge from behind a stone pillar. He must also have been spying on the lovers. His face was pale and twisted with rage and his dark reddish hair, carefully arranged to hide a bald spot, was dishevelled. He had torn off his ruff which was hanging forlornly from his doublet.

Later, one of the servants told me that Don Giulio hated the Duke of Andria. They had once fought a duel over a woman and both had been wounded. It was true that dalliance was common among the lords and ladies of Naples - indeed it was the chief occupation for many. As long as the lovers were discreet these liaisons were tolerated and even applauded. But Donna Maria made little effort to be discreet and her husband was not like other men. We would soon learn the truth of that.

7

Lies and Madrigals

My lady could not stay silent for long. By the fourth day she had poured out the whole story, knowing that I could be relied on to say nothing to anyone. She and the duke were lovers. They met whenever they could.

'There is nothing we can do, Laura,' she said in a silly, dreamy voice. 'I would do anything for him, but I shall need your assistance.'

Of course, I would help her. I was her body servant and I had sworn to serve her in everything. That did not mean that I was happy about it. I feared for her and I feared for my own neck if the prince discovered the truth. Only his disinterest in his wife and his obsession with his music prevented him from seeing what was obvious to everyone else.

For weeks after we returned to Naples I ran between the lovers with perfumed notelets, kept watch at chamber doors, and lied to my master with terror in my heart. I was convinced that those black, fathomless eyes could see through me but he accepted whatever excuse I offered.

Briefly, we returned to the castle of Gesualdo and one day I went to the music room with some refreshments for the prince. This was unusual. His pages provided these services, his pretty boys, but the cook thrust a tray into my hands and told me to hurry. I held my breath as I entered the room but he did not even look up.

The music room was a welcome place on that cool autumn day. A fire was blazing and the sweet smell of apple wood, pine and chestnut logs filled the room, drifting up to the carved, vaulted ceiling. As well as the musical instruments and the sheets of music lying on small tables there was the gleam of ruby wine in a carafe and a small mountain of fruit lying on a silver platter.

A day bed was placed at one end of the room covered with red and gold brocade over plump cushions. The room was aglow with tones of red and silver and the blues and greens of a tapestry hanging over the bed, all reflected in the soft firelight.

Through a narrow window I caught a glimpse of the wonderful view – the soft green hills of Irpinia, and across the valley the thread of the Fredane River. It was not surprising that the master spent most of his time here, except for his early morning hunting.

'Place it there and leave me.'

I was thankful that he had not looked at me, that he could not see my lying eyes. He was composing a madrigal dedicated to a mosquito. Carnero told me that afterwards.

As I left the room and scurried along the upper corridor I heard footsteps behind me. I turned as Bardotti seized me, thrusting his beefy, red face close to mine.

'So what was the Sicilian ice-maiden doing in the master's chamber? I would not have thought you were to his taste!' He attempted to kiss me as I thrashed and kicked at him. My boot found its mark and he collapsed with a growl of anguish. As I ran off he called out, 'You'll pay for that, you slut.' Several further oaths followed me as I rushed away.

Three months later we were back at San Severo and Donna Maria confessed that she was with child. She was surprisingly calm about this. 'I have spent some time in my husband's bed, Laura. I am not entirely stupid. He suspects nothing.' Then she smiled her angelic smile. 'Look at you girl; have you been struck by lightning or the Holy Spirit?' It was true; I had sunk to my knees as she spoke and I realized that I was mouthing prayers to the Blessed Virgin and any saints that I deemed useful in this situation. Seconds later I could not remember what I had said.

Donna Maria was untroubled. She was still utterly in love with the duke. Many noble ladies had their paramours and managed to avoid problems with their spouses. The thrill of secret assignations, hidden letters and all manner of romantic deceits also appealed to her. I had never seen her so joyful. This was all very well but the prince was not one of her complaisant Sicilian husbands. Surely, she understood that?

'I will tell my lord about the child tonight,' she said firmly. Then she wavered a little 'or perhaps next week.' We both knew what she meant. Everything depended on her husband's mood. In the event the announcement was made in more dramatic circumstances than she planned.

My mistress sent a note to her husband excusing herself from one of the many musical dinners that she found so tiresome. She pleaded a headache, "a general feeling of lassitude." Perhaps the excuse was genuine, or perhaps she planned another tryst with the duke. Whatever the reason, the excuse enraged him.

He stormed into her chamber screeching in his high-pitched voice and almost spitting with rage. He had composed a new madrigal which was to be played for the first time that evening. His wife was expected to attend. Donna Maria cowered against the wall as he screamed.

'Bitch! Why do you defy me?' He raised his arm to strike her and without thinking I threw myself between them, shouting,

'Don't strike her, my lord, she is with child.' He dropped his arm at once and looked down at me as I lay on the floor. Then he stepped over me.

'Is this true, madam?' She nodded, holding her arms across her chest for protection.

'I was waiting for an opportune moment to tell you, my lord.'

The prince arranged his features in an imitation of a smile. I watched from the floor as he took her hand and kissed it saying, 'This is blessed news indeed. Of course, you must rest.' He left the chamber without another word, stepping over my prone body once more. I lay there until the sound of his footsteps died away. My lady remained braced against the wall.

Life was quieter for the next few months. Once again, I

ran to and from the convent of the Poor Clares for her favourite sweetmeats. The prince troubled her little and the duke managed some midnight visits.

The birth of little Don Alessandro was duly celebrated at the palace with the aristocracy of Naples calling to offer their congratulations and gifts for the infant. The Viceroy sent a miniature spoon and fork in beaten gold.

The duke appeared with some friends wearing his familiar blue and green colours - the peacock lover. He behaved discreetly and offered a suitable gift.

The prince thanked them all and asked them to listen to a new madrigal composed in honour of the child. This was received with disdain by many who did not think it was a suitable activity for a gentleman. As always, the servants were watching from various hiding places.

I was in the chamber a few days later when the duke appeared. The master had gone hunting. The duke held his son tenderly in his arms. I wondered whether the baby was indeed his, but Donna Maria had no doubt.

'Look, Laura, he has his father's long black lashes.' He was indeed a beautiful baby, but Don Emanuele was also a handsome child who did not resemble the Gesualdo family at all, so it proved nothing.

The duke gave my lady a secret gift after the birth, a tiny gold enamelled book cover that hid a cameo portrait- his own portrait. Sometimes, greatly daring, she wore it when the prince was away hunting. There were spies everywhere, answering to their master. Bardotti the valet was their leader.

Within weeks the lovers resumed their affair as passionately as ever, not attempting to hide it from their friends. Everyone in Naples knew of the liaison except the prince, according to the servants, but there were so many scandals circulating in the city. My lord had not been informed by Bardotti. Afterwards I wondered about that. Perhaps even his faithful valet cringed from bearing such news.

When I asked Carnero about the situation he told me that he knew all about the liaison, as did all the servants, but it was never mentioned. Everyone liked Donna Maria and feared Gesualdo. Bardotti was universally disliked.

'I take care never to make jokes about cuckolded husbands!' Carnero grinned and made horns with his fingers.

Prince Carlo Gesualdo had numerous uncles. One was Cardinal Alfonso Gesualdo who visited occasionally, but not as often as Don Giulio Gesualdo. I knew that he lusted after his nephew's wife. I had seen it for myself at the grotto in Chiaia. I was sent to lie for Donna Maria when he visited. 'My mistress is unwell, with her dressmaker, her confessor,' anyone.

If Don Giulio could not see my mistress he spent time with his nephew. They were often closeted together for long periods. Even Carnero was not privy to their conversations. The prince was much influenced by his uncles and I wondered uneasily what that unpleasant little man was saying about my mistress.

My life became one long sequence of lies and sometimes I could scarcely bear it. Then I would run out of the palace and wander the streets of the city to clear my head. Silvia Albano was left to take over my duties with an ill grace.

8

A Warning

On one particular day, I wandered in the narrow streets of Naples that led down towards the bay drinking in the smells and the chaos, the paradise of noise and colours. The streets were again thronged with people despite the plague fears. Beggars, food sellers and servants, donkeys and mules laden with silk or produce for the food stall crowded around. How I loved cities! The smells of coffee, bread, laundries, nuts and roast barley, food cooking in sizzling oil and the cries of the water carriers.

I still hated the depths of the countryside with a passion. The memories of my Sicilian childhood were always there, submerged beneath my busy everyday life, but rising to the surface to torment me at odd moments. The countryside meant poverty and desperation, a lonely, unloved childhood - and Guido Lotti.

By the time I reached the lower level of streets I was hot and tired and wished for a cool drink of lemonade but I had no money. An old crone in a red shawl was selling cherries at the end of the alleyway and the sight of the scarlet and cream fruit glistening in the sun gave me a pang of yearning I could barely control. I watched as a passing housewife bought some fruit and gave the old woman a coin. She replied by calling down a torrent of blessings on the giver's descendants down through the centuries.

The street was deserted when I reached her. As I passed her, slowly and unwillingly, she reached out a surprisingly plump arm and pulled at my skirt. I tried to draw away.

'You look as if you need a drink,' she croaked. 'My house is nearby. Come home with me.' My first reaction was to shake off her hand and run, but it was too hot. The old woman took my hand and turned it over, palm upward. 'I can tell your fortune, girl. No charge…I like your face.'

She stood up and I helped her to carry the basket of cherries. She led me to a nearby tenement and inside I glimpsed a room with a small iron bed, a goldfinch in a cage and a shrine to the Mater Dolorosa with her little lamps. Inside, the woman crooned to the bird and told me to sit on the bed while she poured orzata, barley water, into a cup for me. From beneath the bed she produced a small, cloth-wrapped package containing the tarrochi – the tarot cards.

'You're a gypsy,' I said accusingly, but she just smiled.

'My mother was a gypsy; she knew the secrets of the Egyptians.'

'And your father?' I asked.. She laughed. The croaking voice had gone and she looked much younger and prettier than before. 'He was a priest!' We both laughed as she spread the cards out on the ragged bedcover. Before continuing she seized my hand once more and peered closely at it before dropping it quickly, making a small, inarticulate noise in her throat.

She sat looking down at her hands for a long moment. 'What are you waiting for?'

The woman looked up and gave a forced smile. 'We need more refreshment.' As if from nowhere she poured frothy red wine into my cup and produced slices of a delicate vanilla pastry. I tried to hide my amazement. How could a beggar woman afford such things?

Stogliate was a favourite sweetmeat of my lady's and I had often been sent to the convent of the Poor Clares to buy it for her. I knew the cost and I knew that only the rich could afford such delicacies. This woman was obviously a thief and probably a witch, but I had no money, nothing she could possibly want.

'My name is Fillide,' she said as we ate. 'Tell me who you are.' I found myself pouring out my life story, unable to stop. Fillide showed no emotion as she listened but her fingers moved ceaselessly over the cards.

'Your hand is a very bad one,' she said at last. 'There is violence and death at several points on your lifeline, in the past and in the future. Now we must see what the cards say.' I explained that my life was now bound up with Donna Maria's and I feared for her safety.

'You should leave her. No good will come to you through her.'

My stomach churned so that I almost threw up the wine and the rich pastry.

'I have told you,' I said desperately. 'She saved me when

I was little more than a child, took me into her service. I have been faithful to her and she has always treated me kindly. I vowed in that sanctuary in Noto to serve her always.' Fillide shook her head and grimaced. 'Please don't look like that,' I begged. 'How can I break a solemn vow?' I could see that she did not understand my devotion to Donna Maria. She regarded me seriously saying, 'You are simply in her service. You can find another mistress.'

I watched as she gathered up the cards and shuffled them. Placing them face down she told me to choose three and place them face up on the bed cover. I saw that I had chosen the Magician, the Emperor and the Lovers.

Once more Fillide sat silently staring at the cards then she hummed a tuneless note under her breath, rocking herself to and fro. She seemed to have forgotten my presence and I grew uneasy again. It was time I returned to the palace. Suddenly, she seized my hand in a grip that made me shriek with pain.

'Blood!' She muttered, 'so much blood.'

'No...no!' I cried. 'You must be mistaken, try another card.' Fillide released my hand and picked up the card of the Magician, thrusting it under my nose.

'Can't you see, foolish girl? This means trickery, deceit. Be careful where you place your trust.' She pointed at the Emperor's card. 'There is the man, the tyrant who will bring you harm, you and the one you love.' Lastly, she picked up the card of the Lovers, holding it as if she could feel vibrations from it, as if the card was somehow alive.

'A love affair, yes; tempestuous and stormy. There is great danger here, a choice to be made.'

'Please take another card,' I begged. Again, she laid out the cards called staves face down on the bed cover. She began to count them backwards and turned over a card showing the five of wands or staves, waving it in my face.

'You see? It's all bad. This card indicates quarrels, aggression, a far-reaching deception.' I bowed my head feeling wretched.

'It refers to my lady, doesn't it?' Fillide turned her head away and spoke to the wall.

'Leave your employers…leave this woman. Go far away. Your hand is full of blood.'

I stood up and put on my shawl. 'I must go now. Thank you for your kindness, for your warning, but I cannot leave her.' She gave a faint smile as I left, her face grown young and smooth: 'I will be here when you have need of me,' she called out softly. 'Only five days…there are only five days left.'

9

The Fifth Night

When I entered the courtyard of San Severo I saw a horseman clattering out of the gate with his page. It was Don Giulio Gesualdo once again. He bent down from his horse and dropped a small scroll of paper at my feet.

'Give this to your mistress.' He spurred on his animal raising a cloud of dust that blinded me. I picked up the scroll and went to my lady's rooms feeling more frightened than ever. Had my mistress refused to receive him again?

I found Donna Maria sitting in front of her mirror embroidering a jacket for Don Alessandro. She was in an angry mood which must have been the result of Don Giulio's visit.

'Yes, I received that man but I will contrive somehow never to do so again,' she muttered, eyes flashing. To make matters worse the duke had been called away to his country estates for a few days. These separations were unbearable for my mistress.

'Where have you been? I was asking for you.' She sounded annoyed. 'Silvia never understands my needs.' She stood and paced around the floor of the chamber, still seething. I handed her the letter wondering why Don Giulio had not delivered it in person.

She held the scroll at arm's length as if it gave off a bad smell, her pale cheeks turning pink with anger.

'He has written that if I do not yield to him he will be revenged. The man is deluded and deranged. I wish I could become a man for a few hours, Laura. I would cut him down.' She threw the letter to the ground.

I had not meant to speak of my encounter with Fillide, but I suddenly felt an urge to warn Donna Maria once more even though I knew it would do no good. I told her everything, the cards, the blood prophecy. It was all there in my hand.

'She told me to flee from you,' I said, sinking into an exhausted heap on the floor.

Donna Maria did something she had never done before. She took a silver goblet of wine from the table and poured two thimblefuls of her favourite sweet wine, Lagrime Christi. She offered one to me – her servant! If only my father and my brothers could see me now, drinking wine with the nobility.

My lady produced a letter from her sleeve. 'You must know Laura that the duke wished to break off our affair because of the danger to me from all the gossip in the city. I told him I would rather die with him than live without him. This letter is his reply. He has promised to do whatever I wish.'

I shuddered; had she not understood anything I said? I

rose and lit a candle, carefully burning both pieces of paper.

For the next few days Donna Maria became extraordinarily preoccupied with her jewels. We sorted and re-sorted them into piles, pearls here, rubies there, gold and emeralds - each one placed in a marked box. I was given a gift of three beautiful milk-white pearls, each the size of a fava bean. 'These will be your dowry one day, Laura,' she said, kissing me on both cheeks as she pressed the box into my hands.

I wept uncontrollably afterwards in my own quarters, misery clutching at my head and heart as I smoothed the pearls with my fingers. All I could think of was Fillide's warning, "So much blood!"

It was because of my pre-occupation with the jewels that I failed to notice what was happening in the palace. Of course, I blame myself for this as I blamed myself for so many things afterwards. I was spellbound by the pearls having never been given anything so magnificent. I do not know what I could have done. I only know I would have tried to save her.

There were many workmen in the palace banging and clattering in the corridors, fitting new bolts on the doors. The iron ones were replaced with wooden ones which failed to close properly. I thought little of this at the time. If only my brain had not been so slow. Bardotti was overseeing the work.

On the fourth morning, the prince appeared in the chamber to announce that he was going to be away hunting for a few days. These were the first words he had spoken to my lady for ten days. She said that he had only played "eerie songs" in her presence and given her evil looks.

'I fear he has discovered the truth, Laura.' She sounded quite calm about it while my knees began to shake.

'You must leave the palace immediately, my lady. Seek sanctuary with the duke somewhere while the prince is away.' Donna Maria shrugged her white shoulders and tossed her head.

'That is not possible. We are outcasts now. I am not ashamed; have we not declared that we would rather die together than live apart?' I walked out of the room so that she would not see my tears. How could she ignore the character of her husband, his wicked mind? Surely she did not really want to die? Soon after, I was told to deliver a note to the duke arranging an assignation for the following night.

When I remember that night I recall mainly the stillness in the air, as if the very heavens held their breath waiting for some terrible event. At ten o'clock my lady was resting on her bed pretending to read a book.

If I close my eyes I can see that great gilded bed with its scarlet hangings. The bed head was carved with scenes from the Greek myths and a statue of a nymph stood at each corner surmounted by a crown.

What became of that bed? Is it stuffed in an attic with its silk rotting and the mattress slit and filthy as if it had some foul disease, tainted as it was by blood and terror? The prince would never have kept it among his possessions.

I sat outside the room sewing the three pearls into my underclothes for fear they would be stolen. If only I had not been so absorbed in my own affairs - but would it have made any difference?

As soon as my lady heard the duke's call she admitted him through the window. I went in to light the candles and to pour them some wine at my mistress's command. The duke smiled at me and wished me 'good evening.' He was one of those rare aristos who noticed servants.

The lovers were already pulling off their clothes as I left the chamber. My lady's bed gown glimmered white in the candle light where I had placed it carefully across a chest. She waved me out, allowing the duke to assist her.

Once outside the chamber I poured a little wine for myself to calm my agitated spirit. I sensed that Donna Maria was also nervous. Normally she drank little.

I left them to their few hours of pleasure before they must have fallen into a deep sleep. I also fell asleep so that I failed to warn the duke to leave. We were not to know that Bardotti had drugged the wine, as his master had ordered. Don Giulio had told the prince everything and the changing of the locks had been part of the trap laid for the lovers.

I woke when I received a violent kick from the accursed Bardotti. I fell against a wall as he stood there holding a flaming torch together with a group of armed men jingling and clashing with weapons. In the midst of them stood our master armed with his pugnello, the dagger carried by prince and commoner alike. His black eyes shone a mad, glowing red in the torchlight.

I watched, paralysed, as the door was thrown open and the men burst in. The sound of screams and shouts and obscenities whirled around me as I sat there, my legs refusing to move. It was only when the prince ran out clutching the dagger, now stained with blood that I fully realized what had happened. He did not see me - or anyone. He was in his own private hell. He muttered, 'I do not believe she is dead!' before rushing back into the room.

I glimpsed the chamber through the open door for a second that could have been an eternity. I saw a figure dressed in my lady's white silk gown with the black embroidery on the sleeves. The white silk was striped with crimson and my lady's head was at an unnatural angle. Except that it was not her blonde curls hanging down, but the duke's long black hair. They had dressed him in her bed gown. His body was held upright supported by the halberds that pierced it and skewered it to the floor. I could not look at the bed where I knew she was lying naked.

I could smell the fetid odour of the chamber pot overlaid with the sharp coppery tang of blood and the sweating soldiers. The taste of terror was in my mouth.

Then fear gave wings to my feet and I fled down the narrow wooden stairs through long corridors and wide salons, blindly seeking a small door that was seldom used. It opened onto a side street outside the palace.

I leaned against a wall, sweating, gasping and crying with only that eerie stillness, that supernatural hush around me as if all of Naples had fallen asleep forever. A sudden cry forced my legs into motion and I ran blindly away through the streets towards the bay, seeking Fillide's house. When I banged at her door it opened quickly and she dragged me in, bolting the door behind me.

'I was expecting you,' she said. 'It is the fifth night.'

10

Exile

I lay on Fillide's bed all that night while she sat in a chair watching and soothing me as I wept and sobbed and shuddered until I fell into an uneasy sleep just before dawn.

During the weeks that followed the walls of that stuffy little room closed in on me until I believed I was in my tomb and I screamed in agony for release. Then, sometimes the walls would disappear completely and I was whirling through space in darkness with only the cold stars and planets for company. Sometimes I knew that Fillide was there. Occasionally I swallowed a little soup. Most of the time I just lay on the bed lost in misery and my nightmares.

When I eventually regained my senses, I sat up on the bed listening to the canary trilling, marvelling at my own arms and legs grown thin as sticks, overwhelmed by the sunlight slanting down from the high window. When Fillide returned she persuaded me to eat a little while she told me what had happened in my absence.

'Oh yes,' she smiled,' your body was here but your spirit was far away. Now, I hope you can recover.'

The murders were the talk of Naples. The prince had ordered the bodies to be thrown into the piazza in front of the palace. Donna Maria's body had received forty stab wounds. Fillide lowered her voice and leaned towards me. 'It is said that a passing friar used the body of Donna Maria even though she was dead.' I buried my head in my hands as she continued.

'They were disposed of as you would dispose of a dog. The nobility and the Viceroy were outraged. The corpses of the nobility can't be treated as if they were common criminals!'

I nodded, 'Especially as the Viceroy is Donna Maria's uncle.'

'The prince was summoned to the court. Witness statements were taken. Your name was mentioned as a witness,' Fillide said. 'A search was made for you while you were lying here.' I curled up into a ball of terror on the bed but she soothed me once more. 'It's all over; sentence has been given. You need not be afraid.' I looked up at her, hope rising in me again.

'You mean he's dead...the prince has been executed?' She gave a peal of laughter;

'Executed? Of course, he wasn't executed. He is a noble with powerful relatives. His uncles at the Vatican pleaded for him. He has been exiled to his country estate for a long period. That is all.' I shook my head until it ached and wept until my body could not produce any more tears..

'Two lives are worth nothing, then, just an extended holiday in the country? Santa Maria! The heavens are blind and deaf.' But I already knew that.

Fillide shrugged. 'Wife-murder is not such a terrible crime in this country. As for the duke, that is a different matter, I think. Gossip in Naples says that his family will kill the prince. The Carafas are a powerful clan.'

'Please God!' I muttered. Then another terror grabbed my mind. 'The prince will search for me. I saw everything. He will not rest until I'm dead.'

'Nonsense, why should he do that? He has admitted his crimes and received his punishment. What can you say that would make things worse for him?'

'I know him, I know his vengeful nature. He knew of my love for my mistress. I came with her from her previous life'. That would be enough to make him hate me, but the prince seldom needed an excuse. 'I tell you, he will want me dead.' Fillide could not convince me otherwise but as I grew stronger she distracted me with talk of what I could do. I could not stay with her forever. She was poor and needed to work to eat. I would have to find employment but the thought of leaving that room was terrifying.

When I eventually summoned the courage to leave the house I found that my friend was right. Nobody from the Viceroy's court was looking for me and there was no sign of anyone from the Gesualdo household. They had all gone into exile with him, if a lengthy stay in the country could be called exile.

I discovered that my poor mistress's tomb was in the church of San Domenico Maggiore, the same church where all Naples had witnessed her marriage.

One day I gathered my courage together and crept into the church with my head well covered. I knelt in the huge transept afraid to enter the chapel where the tomb lay. After my prayers and a promise that I would avenge her, I crept back to Fillide's house, shuddering as I passed the Palace of San Severo. What a fool I was. How could anyone who was such a coward be an instrument of revenge?

Bitterness overwhelmed me as the weeks went by. I was still living on Fillide's charity, helping her when I could, selling fruit and assisting when she read the cards to local women. One day she announced that we should leave Naples.

'I've had enough of this city,' she declared. 'Let's go to Rome; we can seek our fortune there.'

'Rome?' I quaked at the thought. I was a country bumpkin at heart. What would I do in Rome? Fillide waved my objections aside.

'I have been in Rome once or twice with my people.' She meant the gypsies. 'It is much smaller than Naples, but much richer. We will do well there, wait and see.'

My mind was made up when Carnero, the prince's dwarf, found me selling fruit in the market. He had always been my friend and now he was one of the few servants permitted to come into Naples. He was eager to tell me all the gossip.

'My musical, murdering master is amusing himself in the castle at Gesualdo. Sometimes he grows very depressed and black humoured. His conscience is beginning to trouble him. He talks of building a church to atone for his sins.' Carnero chuckled and waved his short, twisted legs in the air. We were sitting on a bench outside a tavern. I played with the oranges in my basket.

'Does he ever mention my name?' Carnero shook his head. 'Once only, after the murders when he noticed you were gone. He was told you had run off and I think he forgot about you. He had much on his mind.' The little man suddenly covered his face with his hands and then looked up at me. 'He may well have a guilty conscience. No amount of church-building will atone for what he has done.' I nodded and a few tears trickled onto the oranges. 'My poor mistress,' I sighed,and the poor duke.' I remembered the handsome, peacock nobleman.

Carnero stared at me. 'There is something even worse; haven't you heard?' I shook my head, dreading what I would hear. 'The baby, Don Alessandro.' 'What?' I gasped. Tears filled the dwarf's eyes as he gazed at me.

'The prince had the baby killed. He believed the child was the "duke's brat" as he told everyone.' My throat was suddenly as dry as a summer wind.

'How?'

'The baby's cradle was suspended by ropes from the balcony at the castle. Bardotti and a few others were commanded to rock the cradle vigorously for a few days and nights until the baby died of suffocation. While they did this the master commanded his singers and musicians to sing madrigals about the beauty of death.' The poor babe! I remembered the gold christening cup he had been given. In view of his fate, a winding sheet would have been more suitable.

Carnero let out a dry sob and both of us were soon

weeping uncontrollably. Passers-by regarded us curiously and some found the sight amusing.

When we had recovered a little Carnero added that the baby's nurse had lost her mind after being forced to watch the execution. 'For that was what it was, Laura - the execution of a baby.' I mopped my tears and said,

'How can you serve a man like that?' He shrugged and waved his legs again.

'Look at these! How can I live except by amusing men like the prince?' That was the heart of the matter. How can the poor live? I told him that Fillide and I were leaving for Rome. He nodded in agreement, telling me I should leave Naples and its terrible memories.

'Make a new start, Laura. We will meet again, I'm sure.' I could not stop myself from blurting out, 'I will kill him. I will avenge my mistress.'

'And I will help you if the chance presents itself,' Carnero grimaced; 'and so would many others if we could do it and keep our heads on our shoulders.' When I returned to Fillide's house I told her everything.

'You are right, my friend. We should leave this place.' She gave a little smile; 'It is spring and time to move.'

11

Extract from the Journal of
Carlo Gesualdo, Prince of Venosa

May 3.1593

My valet, Bardotti, tells me that there is still much talk in Naples regarding the murders of my wife and her lover. My name is denigrated by my peers, but I care little. I consider that the Viceroy has treated me fairly, considering that he is my wife's uncle. As for the Carafa family, I do not fear them. Let them threaten and rage as they will...

12

The Cards Never Lie

Once again, things did not go according to plan. A man called Aldo Pretti was responsible for that. Although we had become close in a few short months, almost like sisters, I did not really understand Fillide. Sometimes I found her in a trance-like state that filled onlookers with fear. Afterwards she would laugh it off.

'It's just a performance; I give them what they want, but I tie my advice up in knots like a true sibyl.' She laughed, but I knew she had a genuine gift. Had she not predicted the tragedy at the palace on the fifth night?

Our rooms were always full of friends and clients. Gypsy women would dance wild tarantellas with Fillide. Sometimes I would join in with the dancing. Men came too; tawny skinned, trinketed strangers, clad in gaudy rags and hung about with many chains and rings. The women, like my friend, wore their raven hair in tiny plaits with necklaces of amber and coral beads and gold coins. Their clothes were bright but tattered, and their eyes were full of sullen Egyptian mystery.

Occasionally, wealthy merchants would come. Their

excuse was to have a card reading. Would the wind be fair for their ships…would the voyage be a profitable one? Aldo Pretti was one of the merchants. His reason for visiting was to share Fillide's bed. He wooed her with gifts of rare fruits, sweetmeats and lengths of silk brought from his ships.

'Can he be trusted?' I asked her.

'Who knows? Few men can be trusted, my pet, but his gifts are good enough and we should enjoy them.'

The merchant owned ships that traded between Naples and Malta and beyond to the shores of a place called Africa - a country full of dark people, cursed by God. Sometimes I would see these people near the port with their black skin hidden by white robes and scarves. I wondered if there were unicorns in Africa.

Fillide saw her follower two or three times each week whenever he could escape his wife's vigilant eye. Like many men he admired my friend's brilliant colouring, her shining black hair coiled around her head and her clear tawny eyes and amber skin. Those eyes were sometimes green like the sea and sometimes gold like an animal. "Wolf eyes" they would have called them in Sicily.

Aldo Pretti was fat with eyes that were too close together. When he laughed everything rippled and trembled, his jowls, his lips, his belly – even his hair. Fillide did not appear to mind her admirer's lack of beauty. Bodies were just bodies to her: she always looked into people, searching for some hidden quality. I could not see that Pretti's inner qualities were any finer than his outer casing, but I was not looking through my friend's eyes.

It was because of her involvement with Pretti that we delayed leaving Naples. We still talked of going to Rome but Fillide knew that her lover would not take the news well. He was a jealous man with a ready temper.

'What is she doing here? Get rid of her.' These words greeted me whenever he came to the house and I would disappear obediently.

One evening in August I went with Fillide to a tavern where many people knew her. The burning heat of the day had given way to a star-studded hot night that wrapped around us like folds of soft black velvet. The streets and taverns were swarming with people and for the first time in many months I drank, laughed and relaxed in public. Fillide danced wildly like a woman possessed. We stayed late into the night and left with an escort of drunken acquaintances. As we stumbled out I thought I caught a glimpse of Aldo Pretti. He was far from his familiar territory and the expression on his full moon face had not been pretty.

In the following days, I often found Fillide poring over the cards with an anxious expression. Then she would throw herself onto her bed with her face set in drawn, angry lines. Without speaking she set out the cards again. I watched anxiously as her face darkened.

'What is it?' I begged. 'Tell me what is wrong.' She shrugged and put the cards away and we prepared a meal. When I found her weeping quietly I made her tell me what was wrong. 'I will help you as you helped me.' She gave a harsh laugh and threw a card into my lap.

'There is nothing you or anyone can do. This card means

death. Sooner or later, next week or in six months' time. There is nothing to be done.'

'Don't say that. You told me that things are not always clear to you.' She shook her head.

'That card never lies. Death is death.' I began to shiver as I remembered my last night in Gesualdo's palace.

After that revelation Fillide was often away from home and I was busy at the convent where I had gained employment in the laundry. Fillide became more reckless – dancing and singing in the taverns every night. I wished I could be more like her, until I remembered Aldo Pretti.

One evening, suddenly, she told me that she was leaving for Rome without me. The merchant had business there for several weeks and he wanted her company. I stared at her in dismay as she twisted her hands together.

'But you care nothing for him. Why did you agree?' She shrugged and laid out the cards again, her shoulders sagging.

'Something terrible is going to happen to me. I told you.'

'That's because you are leaving with Pretti. Harm will come to you in Rome with that man.' She shrugged again.

'It's as good a place as any for a gypsy witch.' Fillide lifted another card and gave a dry sob. 'Always the same card – look! It means death,I cannot escape my fate.' She looked at me, her eyes glowing with green fire. 'You can't come with us. He will not allow it. Stay here in Naples. You will be safe now that the prince has gone. It will be better for you to be away from me.' I felt a taste like sour lemons in my stomach. Pain made me throw hurtful words at her.

'I thought you were my friend. You took care of me and

now you are deserting me.' I knew I sounded childish and petty. I was a grown woman. I could take care of myself, but Fillide was the only real female friend I had ever had. Donna Maria had been my saviour and my employer but she was too grand to be a friend. I collapsed on the floor covering my face with my hands.

During the night I stirred, feeling as if something had touched my cheek lightly. Was it a ghostly kiss - or had someone walked over my grave? In the morning, I found Fillide gone.

13

A Burning

The sun was high and the bird was singing its heart out as if it knew that its mistress would never return. Acting on instinct, I opened the shutter on the small window and let some morning air into the close atmosphere. The little room that had once seemed like a sweet refuge from the world when Fillide had first invited me there now felt like a dungeon. I threw the little creature out of the window and watched it fly over the rooftops.

'Find her,' I whispered, 'go to Fillide - she's waiting for you.'

I took my few possessions and left the little room forever. I returned to the convent laundry and begged for a place to stay, saying I had been evicted from my lodging. Fortunately, the sisters knew nothing of my connection to Fillide or they would surely have refused me. I had been a good worker and so they offered me a corner of a work room, threw down a pallet of straw and an old blanket and told me I could stay.

I dragged through many weeks in that place, feeling

bereft. My world became a white one filled with damp linen and steam. I went out as little as possible and grew more and more withdrawn. In the night, I would plot revenge against Gesualdo but it was just a fantasy. First, I would have to learn courage from somewhere. Often, I wondered how Fillide was faring in Rome and I prayed that she was wrong about the cards.

When the news came it was as if the messenger had kicked me in the stomach. Her name was Alexia and she was an untidy, snaggle-toothed, loose-limbed creature who was never able to look you in the eye because her own were misaligned. She squinted at me and grinned, waving her hands at the other women to attract their attention. It was lunch time: cloths were being unwrapped and meagre pieces of bread and cheese appeared. Slices of melon and peach were divided up.

Poor Alexia was a harmless creature. I bore her no ill will, but she brought the third great misery into my life. First there had been the rape in Sicily, then the murder of Donna Maria – and now this. Alexia's husband was a carter who often took long journeys with his goods. He had recently returned from Rome and had news that concerned Neapolitans. She was eager to tell everyone.

'They burned that gypsy fortune-teller for a witch. What was her name…Fillide something?' A buzz of interest and excitement followed. Questions rang out as I collapsed quietly onto my straw bed. The room dissolved into darkness and I felt sick and light- headed. Mother of God! They burned her.

Nobody noticed me, white faced and shaking in the corner. In my head, I pictured everything. Once, I had witnessed a burning in Palermo with Donna Maria and her entourage. Many found the spectacle entertaining. The Inquisition was burning a heretic but the kindling had not been dry enough. There was a deal of smoke and the fire had to be re-lit after the victim's legs had burned through but his upper body remained intact. I prayed that he had been suffocated by the smoke before the burning.

The noise made by the crowd was one I shall never forget, a low growling, rumbling sound like an animal. And the stench – the sweet, sickly smell of burning flesh. A bystander had urged everyone to go on afterwards to the piazza reserved for burning sodomites. 'Plenty of sport to be had there!'

I became conscious of the laundry room again as someone asked, 'Who betrayed her to the authorities?'

'The rumours say it was her lover, or former lover,' Alexia told us. The women nodded and sighed and Alexia gave a raucous laugh. At that moment, I could have killed her if I had had any strength in my limbs. The women finished their food and I dragged myself back to my work. It was the feast day of San Corrado, patron of Noto, a day that had always had happy associations for me. That evening I went to pray at Donna Maria's tomb in San Domenico Maggiore, adding Fillide's name to my silent cries.

As I crouched in that palace of red and cream marble and mosaic I saw the gilded, carved escutcheons high on the walls, my lady's family arms among them. The light in the church was growing dim; twilight turned the side chapels into black holes like rotten teeth in a beautiful face. Only one candle was alight before the statue of the Blessed Virgin. Even Saint Dominic was almost invisible. There was total silence except for the loud beating of my heart. I crept out feeling like an ant about to be crushed underfoot.

As I left the church I crossed the piazza in front of San Severo, averting my eyes as I passed. It was as if I had crossed into another world. Suddenly, the still air became thick with acrid smoke and I began to choke. I staggered along barely able to see until the smoke cleared a little.

I saw a slight figure tied to a stake in the middle of the piazza with a strip of leather gagging her mouth. A group of soldiers stood around as some priests instructed them to throw more wood on the pyre. Oh, Santa Maria…it was Fillide! As the blue flames licked the kindling her face showed livid and huge-eyed, staring at something only she could see. A priest thrust a crucifix on a long pole close to her face but she ignored it.

Bile rose in my throat and my hair stood on end. I felt as if I would explode with the horror of it. I longed for one of the soldiers to put her out of her misery with a throw of his dagger but the flames leapt higher and I was driven back by the heat.

And then I found I was standing on the edge of the empty piazza. The air was calm and clear once more; the brief southern dusk was giving way to night and the first stars were appearing. I leaned against a door for support until I had the strength to return to the convent. Donna Maria always said this place was full of ghosts. I remembered her telling me that she had dreamed of watching her own funeral there. This was not long after her marriage to the prince.

'The church was full of shadows,' she told me. 'I saw my body lying on its bier among the winged angels and stone lions. I could smell the incense and hear the chanting of the monks as I was laid in the family tomb.' I shuddered as she described it. Soon after this she began her liaison with the duke.

I knew I had seen a vision because of the silence. The realization came to me moments later. Where were the crowds chanting and calling for blood, the shouts of the executioners, the screams and laughter, the terrible, sweet stench of burning flesh I recalled?

Fillide's burning as narrated by Alexia was the talk of the laundry room for a week or two, although the excitement was far less than when the murder of my lady and the duke took place, I was told. Rome, after all, was far away and Fillide was only a gypsy not an aristocrat. As we threw soiled linen into the vats the other women nodded to each other saying…'That Fillide… she was a witch after all. Still…it was a pity. We don't burn witches here in Naples.' In fact, nobody was burned in this city, not even heretics. The Inquisition had been thrown out by popular consent – for the present at least.

I said nothing. I was numb, like a walking corpse just as I had been after Donna Maria's death. I felt nothing and I hardly ate. All I could think of was how I could be revenged on Aldo Pretti. For the moment that was even more important than dealing with Gesualdo.

During the day, we stood on wooden plinths in order to reach into the cauldrons and stir the clothes with sticks as they were boiled. The chamber was vaulted and painted white; even the rafters from where the cauldrons were suspended were white. We wore white aprons over our clothes and saw each other as ghostly pale shapes through the white mist. Each day I felt more and more detached from the world. How easy it would be to drift away in that steamy air-or to fall into the boiling vats.

Six weeks later my clothes hung on my wasted body and my eyes were starting from my head. I was told to work alone in a corner of the room lest I infected the others with whatever disease I was carrying. I knew that I would die if I ate nothing. I forced a little food past my lips so that I would have the strength to do my work, but I ate less and less and I grew steadily weaker. It was if my body had given up, although my mind still plotted and planned. My life was like a piece of music with one note constantly repeated. Gesualdo would have understood that: he was fond of using a single note, something harsh and strange left lingering in the air.

One morning I was so weak I swayed and almost fell into a cauldron. A woman dragged me back and I leaned against the wall. When nobody was looking I buried my face in a white cambric shirt hanging from the ceiling. The cotton felt cool and clean against my fevered skin. The next thing I remember is lying in the infirmary with a nun bending over me. The sister, who was the convent apothecary, dosed me with various potions then gave me a bowl of chicken soup.

'You will take all of that,' she commanded, 'then you will

begin to recover.' I barely tasted the soup but by the time I had finished it I knew how I could avenge my mistress and Fillide.

14

Hearts and Flowers

I begged the sister to take me on as her assistant. I can't remember what fantastic story I told her that would justify my claim to know something of herbalism. Words poured out of me so eloquently that the nun was amazed. I am convinced that Fillide was working through me at that moment, putting words in my mouth. After I paused for breath, I begged again,

'In Sicily, I could recognize many herbs, sister. I am a good worker, I learn quickly.' If she guessed that I was not being strictly truthful she gave no indication.

'You cannot read or write,' she pointed out. 'How will you learn the correct ingredients?'

I assured her that my memory was excellent and I would learn by rote. When Sister Antony heard that the laundry wanted to be rid of me, thinking that I was contagious or had been cursed with the evil eye, she tutted at such ignorance and decided to take me on to work in the herbarium. It helped that her previous assistant, an elderly nun, was sick and unlikely to recover.

I shut myself in the herbarium and for months I became the most industrious apprentice in Naples. I learned everything that the nun could teach me. I learned how to mix potions for calming teething infants, potions for toothache and elixirs to restore vigour to older men. I crushed powder that would guard against the plague and others that would reduce fever. I measured and pounded and dissolved, memorising everything because I could not write anything down. Sister Antony would repeat the recipes, the quantities, over and over like a prayer or a psalm. This mixture should be stirred over heat for as long as it takes to say an Ave, that herb must be collected at dawn, another in the spring, or by the full moon. I would repeat and repeat the instructions until I knew them as well as I knew the holy mass. I joined some of the other nuns who helped to dry the herbs, open pods and pound the roots needed to make the various concoctions.

In the convent garden, I would help the apothecary to pick herbs where they were carefully cultivated, then dried and stored in the herbarium. Sometimes we made expeditions into the countryside to find rare herbs. Sister Antony could sense where things were growing, what types of soil produced the thing she sought. I privately called her the human truffle hound, remembering the hunts I had watched with my lady.

So it was that I, little Laura Scala, a nobody from Sicily, became a herbalist and a skilled poisoner by accident.. I always sought to use my skills for good when I was able, but I was also prepared to use them for revenge. It is said that poison is a woman's weapon. Men may settle their differences with swords and wars but we have fewer choices.

I stood by Sister Antony's side as she dispensed her potions to the sick, the melancholic, the lovelorn and those who imagined they were sick. Few people realized that I had often mixed the concoctions myself, distilled the roots, separated the oils or boiled leaves in wine. We handed out angelica root to be chewed as a protection against the plague. I mixed artemisia with salad oil to be spread on old men's pates as a remedy for baldness. Tamarinds, senna and syrup of roses were given as purgatives, dried fennel seeds for indigestion. Valerian and asafoetida were much in demand for women's problems.

I tended the fig trees in the convent courtyard with loving care for the fig together with the olive is the king of trees and a sovereign cure-all. The juice of figs boiled in water can relieve afflictions of the mouth and the lungs while a paste of figs crushed in milk can be applied to wounds or mixed with honey as an ointment. Anxious mothers queued for a concoction of fig leaves boiled in water for their child's cough.

Later, Sister Antony told me that I had recovered my strength after she gave me the convent health drink made from figs, juniper berries and boiled water left to macerate for ten weeks. Vats of this wondrous liquid were stored in the still room and dispensed to the people for a good price.

Sometimes servants would call for a few grains of Peruvian bark to enrich the blood of their wealthy masters. The bark was brought from the New World at great expense but the sisters had gold to buy it. When we distilled oil of French lavender (good for stiffness of the joints) Sister Antony would speak of a holy nun called Hildegarde of Bingen who lived in Germany long ago. This Hildegarde wrote a great treatise on herbs and valued lavender especially. The still room would fill with the heavenly scent as we worked and for a few moments my heart would lift.

Of course, as well as learning which herbs and plants were curatives I had to know which ones could kill or cause sickness. I knew that belladonna was highly prized by ladies as an eye brightener but I also knew that it was a powerful poison. Combined with poppy seeds and thorn apple it could not fail. Sister Antony had whispered that this combination was popular in Venice where the Doge kept a school of official poisoners. I often heard her refer to a potion called Venice Treacle - an antidote to snake bite and poison that was worth a king's ransom.

'It is distilled from sixty-four different herbs, roots and flowers,' she said wistfully, as if she longed to concoct such a remedy herself. Once, she told me of a famous garden in Padova in the north of Italy where every known poisonous plant grew. Students from the university in that town studied there, but women, even nuns, were forbidden such knowledge. Sister Antony had procured books from those who knew these things and had taught herself.

How she loved her work! I often thought that the nun regretted having to distribute medicines to the poor at the convent gates. She was not a hard-hearted woman but her attitude to the concoctions she created was almost maternal.

I watched her as she caressed the leaves of a particularly lovely plant, calling it "my beauty" as she pounded ingredients into a bowl, rolling the plant's Latin name on her tongue.

Regarding my own search for a suitable ingredient, I remembered that Fillide had told me about women at the Viceroy's court who had been slowly poisoned by the arsenic contained in the creams and hog's fat used to whiten and preserve their complexions. I did not care for slow acting poisons. I wanted my chosen victims to die quickly and in some agony.

I whiled away many hours pondering on this. I would happily have boiled the prince in oil and Aldo Pretti too, but I considered using hemlock which was favoured in ancient times. Purple was my favourite colour and a purple flower was my eventual choice. A plant, which caused numbness, dizziness, a racing heartbeat and finally, seizures, would serve very well.

By this time Sister Antony trusted me enough to allow me to deliver potions around the city to the wealthy and important citizens as well as to the poor and needy. I knew that one day my opportunity would come. Aldo Pretti's wife sometimes used the convent's remedies. In return, she would leave a little of her husband's rare spices in thanks. One day, when I was near the church of the Gesu Nuovo on an errand for the convent, I saw a fat man with a disagreeable expression descend from his horse. Aldo Pretti had returned from Rome.

It was a simple matter to steal a small quantity of sweet

cinnamon, cloves and other ingredients for a fruit pie. It was even simpler to add my own special ingredient. After several days of keeping watch my opportunity came. The aroma of sweetmeats arose as I boldly entered the Pretti kitchen. The slatternly servants were sitting at the table, half asleep in the steamy atmosphere. Hiding the pie pan under my shawl, I shouted, 'the strolling players have set up a puppet theatre in the next street. If you hurry you will catch a few minutes of the show.' They rushed out, urging me to join them. I sighed and said, 'I must be about the good sisters' business. Some poor soul in pain needs the medicines I am carrying,' I added virtuously as they waved goodbye.

I quickly left the poisoned pie on the table in a prominent position. All that remained was to entice Pretti into the kitchen where he was sure to notice the food. I grabbed a small boy in the street outside and gave him a coin, telling him to inform the master that a messenger from the convent awaited him in the kitchen. I was sure the merchant would be nearby – probably counting his money.

I hid behind the open door and waited until Pretti appeared. My friend's killer appeared puzzled and annoyed when he saw the empty room. He tapped impatiently on the table before he noticed the pie. Taking a spoon, he began to dig into the crust eagerly, no doubt thinking it was a gift from the convent. I watched him from a shadowy corner as he ate. After a few large mouthfuls, he began to gasp for breath. He staggered towards a water jug but he was unable to reach it before falling in a heap on the floor. The merchant twitched and gasped before beginning to convulse. Careless of being seen or heard I ran over to him and shook my fist in his face.

'Die, die!' I cried as his body gave a final shudder and lay still. I gave his fat carcass a final kick before I seized the pie pan and ran. Later, I heard the news of his death from Sister Antony.

'The poor man must have suffered horribly,' she told me. 'But what can you expect if you eat a fruit pie full of powdered aconite?' She gave me a strange look. 'I wonder how he came by such a thing?'

Something changed after Pretti's death. I did not regret killing him. He deserved to die for what he did to Fillide, but I knew in my heart that I had crossed an invisible border. I was now a murderer and I would pay the price in the next world. I no longer took communion and sometimes I thought I glimpsed her, the black robed figure of Fate slipping around a corner, sending me a backward glance from terrible deep-set eyes. Perhaps the figure was not Fate but that Greek goddess, Demeter, who had received my prayer and now returned to claim her due. I remembered the saying in Sicily, "blood washes blood."

Despite everything that was happening to me, I kept in touch with Carnero. We met secretly in Naples and he told me all that was happening in the Gesualdo household. I knew that the prince continued to live at his castle consoled by his music, his horses and his favourite retainers. I learned that the forest around the castle had been cut down for fear of an attack by the Carafa family, that Donna Maria and her baby son were never mentioned and, finally, after four years

I heard that the prince was planning to marry again. Carnero nodded and looked grim.

'The Viceroy will soon give permission for Gesualdo to leave the castle. His exile from society is coming to an end and he has ambitious plans,' Carnero told me. 'He is seeking an alliance with one of the greatest families in Italy. Ambassadors are advancing his suit at the court of the d'Estes in Ferrara.'

'I don't think our musical fiend really wants another wife after his recent experience!' Carnero laughed. 'It is all the idea of his uncle Alfonso, the Archbishop. You can be sure that the Vatican is involved in some way.

'The prince is agreeing because of the musical opportunities in Ferrara. He wants to get his books of madrigals printed and circulated among the musical elite of that city. His fiercest ambition is to be known as a great composer. I have heard him say this so often.' I stared at Carnero unable to believe my ears. Another woman was to be sacrificed for a few strangled notes.

'We will leave for the north in a few weeks. It is all arranged: he will wed Leonora d'Este.'

'I shall follow,' I promised him.

When I told Sister Antony that I was leaving for the north she gave me a shrewd look.

'Use your skills wisely, my child. Remember you risk being accused of witchcraft. Wisdom in women is not to be tolerated.' She gave a cackle of laughter and touched my cheek with her roughened, stained finger. 'Go with God, Laura.' As I made to leave she called me back and said, 'Do

I not recall that you took some spices from our stock without entering the reason in the ledger?'

Not for the first time I wondered uneasily how much she had guessed about Aldo Pretti's death. I forced myself to look her in the eye and make an excuse. She gave me a searching look before turning away and repeating, 'go with God my child.'

There had been a brief commotion about the death, but no-one was blamed. It was decided that a business rival was probably responsible. If Pretti's servants suspected me they kept quiet. They probably hated him. Then it was forgotten. Neapolitans live for the present.

Later, I heard from Carnero that the prince wanted to atone for his sins by building a chapel. How would I atone for mine?

15

A Thing of Shadows

January 12.1593

The chapel of the Capuchins in Gesualdo is almost completed. Surely this act will stand before the throne of God as a sign of my penitence? My sainted uncle has told me as much. Why then did I see the damned woman on the stairs below my bedchamber? She was standing quite still and pointing to the bloody wounds in her chest as I attempted to enter.

I know she is a product of my disordered imagination for I have heard that she has also been seen wandering around the palace of San Severo searching for that wretch Carafa. Why then would she appear to me here in Gesualdo?

The sight of her causes me an extreme agony of mind that I can scarcely convey in words. I was returning to my chamber at dusk when I first beheld her standing in the dim light of the stairwell, a thing of shadows and grey smoke. I could not see her face but I knew instinctively that she was looking up at me. I forced myself to continue climbing the stairs, only to find her waiting by my chamber door.

My entire body turned to ice but I forced myself to move

forward to open the door. When I looked back – and what agony of mind that action caused me – she had disappeared.

Only music keeps her at bay. When I play she cannot come near me. Let Bardotti bring the Melli woman to me this night. The delights of music and of the flesh will distract my mind. I will command more candles to be lit. More light! I must have more light!

Carnero told me that Gesualdo was a man tormented by demons and spirits – as well he might be. As if the building of a church could atone for everything he did.

When the prince's cortege set out for Ferrara in February 1594 I watched from a distance. I carried a small bag containing all my possessions. It was time to set out on the next part of my life's journey, to fulfil my vow to Donna Maria. I had sacrificed one of my three pearls to pay for the journey.

The cortege was very grand with twenty-four mules carrying three hundred pieces of luggage. When the procession had disappeared, I stood on a hill looking over the glorious Bay of Naples. I wondered whether I would ever see it again. Would it be lost to me forever, like Noto?

16

Madrigalia

March 1593

The efforts of my sainted uncle, Cardinal Alfonso Gesualdo, have borne fruit. A marriage has been arranged on my behalf with Donna Leonora d'Este, niece of the Duke of Ferrara. Many blessings will surely come from such an advantageous union.

Don Cesare d'Este will sign the marriage contract today on behalf of his sister. Leonora brings a dowry of fifty thousand scudi – most satisfactory. I have promised her an annual allowance of six hundred ducats and three hundred and fifty thousand ducats in the monies of the King of Naples to our first born.

The court at Ferrara is renowned for its musical excellence and brilliance in the arts. The best singers and musicians in all Italy assemble there. It will be an unrivalled opportunity for me. Scipione Stella has advised me to take my book of madrigals with a view to having them printed in that city. Thus I am well satisfied with events.

I have not seen HER for some time. She has not appeared on the staircase, although I fancy I saw Carafa standing in the courtyard with a spear protruding from his side just as dusk was falling. Rosalia Melli comes tonight.

January 20. 1594

I have today received the following letter from His Majesty.

I received the letter you wrote to me concerning your marriage to the lady Leonora d'Este, cousin of the Dukes of Ferrara and Urbino. And I think it most fine, for the conformity of the parties and their qualities, and in the understanding that it will be favourable for you and your family, so I am most pleased and I will write in more detail to the Cardinal Gesualdo, your uncle.

Phillip 11, King of Spain.

*****

Part Two

17

New Lives for Old

Venice May 18. 1594

I struggled ashore from the crowded barge, clutching my bundle of belongings after the journey from Chioggia. I knew I was in the district of Venice called Canareggio. One of my travelling companions told me this, advising me that work could be found there where many wealthy families lived. 'Although you are not a Venetian,' the woman had added. 'That could be a problem.'

I wandered along the bank of the canal feeling tired, dirty and hungry. The few coins in my purse would barely buy a night's cheap lodging - a meal was out of the question. Occasionally I paused to ask directions, struggling to understand the harsh Venetian dialect, so different from the softness of the southern tongue. Each time I was rewarded with a sneer, a shrug, or the stock phrase, "sempre dritto"-straight on. Inevitably, I would find myself facing a blank wall or at the end of an alley where water lapped at my feet. Venetians enjoyed confusing visitors almost as much as they enjoyed overcharging them.

It was already early evening. I needed to find somewhere to stay or face a cold night in the streets of springtime Venice with its chilly wind and persistent drizzle. The warmth and humidity of the south seemed a thousand miles away.

Two hours later, sheltering under a low stone archway where a tiny shrine to the Virgin drooped faded blue flowers onto the dank stones; I collapsed against the wall overcome with despair.

All the weariness of the last three months rose to overwhelm me. First, there had been the long and agonisingly slow journey from the south that had taken most of the money I possessed. Then there was the terror of the storm at Chioggia and the voyage down the Brenta and across the lagoon. The sight of the alluring beauty of Venice did little to comfort a penniless outsider. Tears slid down my cheeks and I covered my face with the bundle of clothes.

As the evening gloom darkened into night I wondered how I could once have imagined that my good fortune would last forever. Plucked from disaster in Sicily I had enjoyed several years of comfort and safety in a grand household protected by my lady. Now I was back where I belonged, hungry, penniless and homeless. The folly of my grand vow to avenge Donna Maria had ended in futility. At least in Naples I had a roof over my head and enough work to keep me from starvation. Now I was alone in a foreign city where I could barely make myself understood. I had plotted my own downfall.

Extract from the Journal of Don Gesualdo, Prince of Venosa.

I watched as the barge moved slowly into the Grand Canal following sluggishly in the wake of three gondolas. The first sight of Venice from the sea is as magical as travellers say. Gondolas bobbed elegantly past the Dario palace propelled by liveried gondoliers who were poised like dancers on the prows. The rowers executed a manoeuvre with a graceful flick of the wrist, a turn of the body. I clutched the side rail of the barge, fascinated by this spectacle.

Fontanelli, my companion, indicated a palazzo just ahead.

'That is where we shall stay, the Palazzo Venier. Everything has been arranged for your comfort, sire.' I nodded; my mind elsewhere.

'I must engage my own gondolier and barque. I have had enough of this floundering tub. You may advise me on this, my friend.' Fontanelli nodded. *'It will be necessary to negotiate with the Jews in the ghetto district, my lord.*

'I am surprised that such important matters are entrusted to the Hebrews.' Fontanelli shrugged; *'The authorities here give the Jews many freedoms.'*

'Then we will visit them tomorrow, after I have heard Gabrieli's music at San Marco.' The Count reminded me that we were arriving in Venice on Ascension Day, the twenty first of May. Due to the storms in the lagoon the great ceremony when the

Doge married Venice to the sea had been postponed to the following day.

'Then we will watch the ceremony before hearing Gabrieli's music. There will surely be something special for such an important occasion.'

I saw the prince in Venice soon enough.

After a cold night in a church doorway, I got up and forced myself to walk on. Suddenly, I turned a corner and found that I was in the vast area of the Piazza di San Marco with the Basilica in front of me, topped with many domes like something from one of Tasso's poems that my lady would read aloud. Four great, green horses were poised in mid-air on the roof. For a moment, I imagined that they would leap down on to me as I pressed myself against a door.

Gratefully, I crept inside to rest and shelter for a while in the dim light pierced with the glow of gold and mosaics and shining silver lamps. I must have fallen asleep for a few moments. When I woke the organ was playing and the choir was singing. I heard a voice say that they were rehearsing Gabrieli's motet *Omnes Gentes*.

Suddenly, I saw a small group of men walking down the central aisle toward me. I recognised some of them immediately. They were the prince's musicians. A moment later Don Carlo Gesualdo appeared in the midst of the group. I heard his high-pitched tones before I saw his small figure swathed in a long black cloak.

I drew my shawl across my face as that petulant voice declared, 'Where is Gabrieli? Surely he should be here for this rehearsal?' Other voices chimed in reassuringly as the choir increased in volume drowning out their words. This was my opportunity.

If I was prepared to sacrifice myself I had only to slip out of my seat and plunge my knife into the prince's back as he passed. My lady would be avenged. But I was not willing to die at that moment and fear rooted my feet to the floor. I peered through my shawl as the little procession made its way out of the church. I shook for some minutes and I could not control my hands. Eventually, I left the building and wandered into the alleyways.

Mysterious cloaked figures glided silently past and disappeared, rowdy groups of drunken men could be heard approaching. I slipped into doorways and shivered, only to be pushed out by whores who threatened me for being on their patch and sent me on my way.

Later, moonlight gleamed down on me as it had done once before on a road in Sicily. All around me the gentle susurration of moving water and the rustling of foraging rats provided the only sounds, except for the loud rumblings of my empty belly. Without another thought I curled up at the water's edge, too tired to care about the danger. The next moment I had tumbled over into the canal in the darkness, my bundle still clutched in my hand.

Abruptly, the shock of the freezing water returned me to my senses. I began to thrash and scream as I sank into the black water then rose up again, choking and waving my arms. After I had sunk and risen once more I felt a thump on my back and a strong hand seized my flailing arm.

Within seconds I had been hauled into a narrow, swaying black vessel filled with soft velvet cushions.

My last thought was that I was in a gondola, the secretive black boat in which Venetians spent so much of their lives, and which conveyed them to their last resting-place. As I closed my eyes I dimly made out the faint blue light of a small lantern and the outline of a man standing at the prow.

Minutes later I was awake again and wrapped in a warm pelisse. The gondola was still bobbing gently on the water but I realized that it was now moored somewhere. A strong arm was supporting me and a man's voice was urging me to drink as he tried to pour rough red wine down my throat in the semi-darkness. I pushed his arm away, leaned over the side and vomited into the canal. The man laughed and told me that was the best thing to do.

'Now drink the wine and clear all that filthy water from your guts,' he commanded.

I sat up, feebly thanking my rescuer. I had no energy left to tell him that it had been an accident. I had not meant to throw myself into the canal.

'My name is Gaetano,' the gondolier told me, 'and this is my home.'

Once more he hauled me up in my sodden dress and heaved me onto the landing stage. Taking the lantern in one hand and gripping me with the other, he climbed narrow wooden stairs and opened the door into a small, warm room at the top of the house. An old woman sat in a chair near the window mending a shirt by the light of one flickering candle. She looked up in astonishment at the man's bedraggled burden, holding up the candle for a closer inspection.

'What have you brought me, my son?' Gaetano dropped me onto the floor unceremoniously. 'I fished her out of the canal, Mother. She needs help.'

18

The Ghetto

I slept the sleep of the dead that night wrapped in shawls on a dry pallet unaware that Gaetano and his mother were discussing my plight. Later he told me about their conversation while I was recovering and receiving the signora's reluctant hospitality.

'She is a foreigner,' said Signora Giovanelli. 'Why do we need to bother with such people?' She had deduced this much as she spooned hot soup into me while I muttered feverishly about princes and murder.

'She is in some sort of trouble, mark my words. No good will come to us if we shelter her. Also, she is carrying a knife,' the signora added for good measure.

'Of course she's in trouble, Mother' Gaetano replied. 'People do not usually throw themselves into the canal if they are carefree and happy…unless they are drunk.' Later he told me that his father had drowned in just such an accident coming home from the wine shop during acqua alta.

During the next few days I stayed in that little room fed reluctantly by Gaetano's bird-like, boney mother. Her son was very different; quite tall and broad shouldered with dark eyes that glinted with laughter. His straw hat was crammed over a mop of black curls like my own.

Gaetano was gone from morning till night on his gondola. When he returned late on the second night he looked me up and down.

'You are quite passable when washed and combed!' His eyes glinted again as he grinned and sat down beside me, urging his mother to sit with us. We drank sweet wine and discussed my plight. I invented a reason for travelling to Venice and emphasized that I was willing to work. I repeated that my falling into the canal had been accidental. The signora nodded grimly at this. Gaetano looked thoughtful.

He explained that he rented his gondola from a rich Jewish merchant in the ghetto whom he knew to be looking for a new lady's maid for his daughter.

'Jacob da Costa is a fair man. He has always treated me well and he is in good standing in the community, both Jewish and Christian. He would be a useful person to work for.' I said I cared little whether I worked for Christian, Jew or Musselman as long as they paid.

'Perhaps I could put in a word for you,' Gaetano offered, but his mother interrupted quickly.

'You are forgetting that no Christian may remain overnight in the ghetto. She could work there during the day but would have to leave at sundown. A lady's maid would be expected to live in the house.' Gaetano refused to be discouraged. 'There are ways around these rules. I will speak to Sire da Costa.'

Whatever passed between Gaetano and his employer I never found out, but a few days later I was once more rocking gently in the gondola along the Canareggio canal. Gaetano guided me through the maze of streets into the ghetto where the tall buildings seemed to turn in on themselves as if for comfort, and crowds of dark, exotically dressed people thronged the piazzas, buying and selling, promenading and talking.

'Why are the buildings so tall?' I asked.

'The Jews were forced to build their houses upwards because they were not allowed more land to accommodate their people,' Gaetano explained. 'They must stay within the confines of the ghetto.'

The da Costa house was a few yards away from the main square which housed various places of worship for the different groups in the ghetto.

'The da Costas came from Portugal,' Gaetano explained.

I was shown into a room where a slightly stooped man sat at a desk; his grey curly hair formed a halo around his head setting off a lined face with deep-set, dark eyes. He wore rich velvets, and a large diamond ring blazed on his left hand that was half covering the hated red cap worn by Venetian Jews. Most of the people in the ghetto were as finely dressed as the Neapolitan aristocracy.

I tried not to stare, lowering my eyes as Gaetano introduced me and left the room. I twitched nervously at my skirt, aware of my shabby appearance in this room filled with valuable objects.

'Look at me, child,' commanded Jacob da Costa. I

looked up at him cautiously and he gave a slight smile. 'Gaetano tells me you are a stranger in Venice and in some misfortune. He recommends you to me and his judgement is usually sound. What work have you done before you came here?'

I thanked him earnestly and launched into an explanation of my role as Donna Maria's maid but giving the name of another grandee of the city. It occurred to me that the notoriety of the Gesualdo family might have reached as far as Venice. Da Costa frowned, struggling to understand my accent and nodding occasionally.

'My daughter requires a new maid, although she may not be willing to accept you immediately. Sarah is a demanding young woman. I fear I have spoiled her since her mother died.' He passed a hand over his face for a moment before calling for a servant who was dispatched to find the young lady.

When Sarah da Costa swept into the room she came in a cloud of green and gold velvet, shining auburn hair and enough jewellery to ransom a duke. Appearing not to notice me she dropped a curtsey to her father and kissed his cheek, several rows of pearls clinking against the desk as she did so.

Jacob indicated the visitor standing in a corner and Sarah whirled around frowning darkly. After her father had explained quickly that I might be suitable as a maidservant the frown grew even darker and she appeared to swell visibly before preparing to roar. I watched, fascinated, as the red-haired girl launched into a torrent of angry words which indicated that she wanted nothing to do with this ragged creature and would select her own servant. What could her father be thinking of to suggest such a person?

At a convenient moment when the girl paused to draw breath her father replied wearily that I had been a personal maid to a member of the Neapolitan aristocracy. New clothes could easily be provided.

'She is a fortunate find for us, my child. I want no more of your tantrums today, they tire me.' Again, he passed a hand over his face and Sarah instantly ran to his side, full of remorse. After peace had been declared she addressed a few questions to me and stared in horror as the replies came in a strong southern accent.

'How can I be expected to communicate with this creature, father? She is a foreigner, scarcely intelligible.' Jacob frowned angrily.

'You forget that we are also foreigners, my child. We have been shown much kindness in Venice. We should do the same for others. Now be off with you and show the girl her duties - or manage without a maidservant.' Sarah flounced out of the room and I followed her after a nod from Jacob.

We climbed several winding staircases to a chamber that looked out over the piazza and the surrounding tenements towards the bulk of the Church of the Madonna in its orchard. Still muttering angrily to herself, Sarah da Costa rummaged in a cavernous closet and began to throw various items of clothing at me.

'You can manage with these for now. Some of them are things I no longer wear, some of them were left behind by Donatella, my previous maid.' I had the impression that

Donatella had left in a hurry.

Obediently, I removed my shabby clothing and put on clean and surprisingly luxurious items. Even servants and ordinary workers here wore extravagant clothes. Later, Gaetano told me that the Venetians adored their finery and that the Doges were constantly trying to limit these outrageous displays of luxury, with little success.

As I looked around the small room, scattered with costly gowns, I was transported for a moment back to Naples, to Donna Maria's spacious chamber, seeing her nibbling almond biscuits while I re-arranged her clothes and her embroidered slippers, placing pot pourri in burgundy silk bags around the chamber. Sarah's masks lay untidily on the floor. Donna Maria had always lived behind a mask. The mask was her own face and personality, changed whenever it was necessary.

In my mind's eye, I could see the cedar press and smell the scent of strawberries that wafted from my lady's skin when you drew close to her. I remembered how she would wriggle her bare feet in the sunlight, admiring her slender ankles as they peeped coyly from her skirt. Pain gripped my heart for a moment until I came to my senses, aware that Sarah da Costa was looking at me in alarm.

I smiled politely and began to tidy the contents of Sarah's vast wardrobe. I was instructed in the use of zoccoli, the stilt-like wooden clogs worn by Venetian ladies to keep their feet out of the mud and water, and then I was summoned again to Jacob's room. A sum of money was agreed and he told me that I would not be required to sleep in the house. Gaetano would collect me when the gates of the ghetto were closing. I should return early the following morning.

At the end of that first day when soldiers were shouting and hurrying people through the gates I stepped into the gondola anxious to question Gaetano about my living arrangements.

'You can lodge with us.' Seeing the expression on my face he told me not to worry. 'I have arranged everything…do not worry about my mother.' He gave me that disarming grin.

That night, in the little room, the three of us drank fragolino and ate cake that had been left behind in the gondola by careless pleasure-seekers. Through the small window I could see the faint glow of candles and the fiery red of tapers bobbing about on the canal as merrymakers went to their next rout, to the theatre or to their latest assignation. This was a city hell bent on pleasure; its citizens seemed to have no cares.

As I sipped the wine I wondered where the prince might be on this night. Would he be drowning his bitter memories in wine or visiting some of Venice's twenty thousand whores? I did not know how long he would stay in the city and I had no idea of the distance between Venice and Ferrara.

Gaetano's hand brushed lightly across my hair as he reached for more wine. I felt my neck quiver a little. 'You are many miles away, Laura. What are you thinking of?'

'There was a great storm in the lagoon as we approached Chioggia. The journey from the south took so long.' I was aware that I was really talking to myself. He watched my face closely as I added, 'How strange this water city is.'

He nodded, 'Yes, strange and wonderful, as you will discover. Do you know what happened the day after you arrived, while you were still lying in the corner half dead?' I shook my head as Gaetano and his mother burst out laughing.

'That was the day Venice was married to the sea,' cackled the old lady. Seeing my puzzled expression Gaetano explained. 'It happens every year on Ascension Day. The Doge is rowed out into the lagoon on his golden barge where he throws a golden wedding ring into the water to symbolise the city's marriage to the sea.'

'The sea, which is our defence and our mother,' the old lady added.

'All the grandees of the city were present, the ambassadors, hundreds of visitors, the people. The patriarch gave his blessing, choirs sang and I was busy all day, rowing to and from the lagoon.'

I tried to imagine the prince among the throng watching from the balcony of a palazzo on the Grand Canal, or in a gondola on the lagoon. Perhaps Gaetano had taken him in his sleek black coffin? The old lady interrupted these thoughts to ask me about the da Costa household and my duties there. She warned me that I must get up very early to be at the ghetto entrance when the gates opened.

'You can walk from here,' the signora said in her customary sour manner.

Gaetano immediately offered to take me in the gondola

because I was unfamiliar with the narrow alleyways of the city. His mother snorted angrily and prepared for bed. Gaetano grinned knowingly at me and said goodnight. He slept in a narrow alcove outside the communal room. As I drifted off to sleep I saw a funereal gondola bobbing out into the lagoon and I found myself standing on the prow as the gondolier. When I looked behind the black velvet drapes into the felze, the little cabin, I saw the bleached bones of a skeleton wearing Donna Maria's clothes - a dream that would recur often during my time in Venice. Sometimes I saw the prince himself sitting behind the curtains. Once I saw myself on the soft cushions, alive, clutching a newborn baby. I woke with a cry of alarm, puzzled and fearful.

19

Extract from the Journal of Don Carlo Gesualdo

May 24.1594

Today I attended a formal dinner at the Arsenale given in my honour. I hastened to leave early which displeased some of the dignitaries, but the building of fighting galleys interests me very little – and the musical entertainment was poor.

The gentlemen of this city offer me refreshments each day and they have promised me a galley to be kept at my disposal for the return journey. I have been received everywhere with great honour, due, I believe, to the esteem in which my uncle the Cardinal Archbishop of Milan is held.

I dined lately with the Patriarch but the singers and musicians provided for the entertainment were again very poor so that I was obliged to leave the room to remonstrate with them. The director and soloists were much put out by my words. Gabrieli has not appeared yet but I will endeavour to meet him by some means. I have heard that the gentlemen of this city are affronted that I do not rise early enough to attend the tours they prepare for me. I habitually rise at four in the afternoon and I find that ample time for everything I wish to accomplish. I have already composed two new madrigals since I arrived in the city. This pleases me greatly as it will add to my esteem at the court of Ferrara.

At supper, this evening, I will send for a cembalo so that I can play for Fontanelli and also accompany Scipione Stella. I shall make a point of being served in the grand Spanish style, having the lighted torch brought in before the cup and covering my plate while I drink, as befits a true gentleman.

I plan to visit Gardone to arrange for the printing of my books of madrigals. I have found the singing in the churches here to be of poor quality.

May 26. 1594

Fontanelli and his Venetian acquaintances arranged a diverting evening for me. We went across the lagoon to the island of Mazzorbo where we visited the convent of Santa Caterina. Young noblemen, such as Lorenzo Marin, who accompanied us, like to divert themselves in this way. The noble daughters of Venice, young, beautiful and wealthy, are often sent to the religious life to avoid the expense of their dowries. They live in considerable grandeur, contriving to maintain their former standard of luxury as far as possible. They entertain visitors and sometimes take lovers, according to Marin, who boasts that he has had more than one holy sister as an inamorata. This is possibly true, but the Church and the Council of Ten impose severe penalties for such activities if discovered.

We set out to reach the island by early evening where the good sisters welcomed us warmly, offering wine and all manner of sweetmeats. Some of the younger nuns performed a masque for us accompanied by male musicians - all strictly forbidden of course. Marin and the others flirted madly with the women, but I preferred to save my energies for later when I planned to visit one of the city's fairest and most expensive whores.

One of the loveliest of the sisters wore rich silks and contrived to raise the hem of her skirt in order to display a shapely leg clad in silk edged with gilt lace. Fontanelli told the abbess that I was a composer and she expressed a wish to hear one of my compositions. I took a lute from one of the musicians and played a madrigal to gratifying applause.

On the return journey Marin told me that the nuns were wont to use glass dildos made for them on the island of Murano. He claimed to have arranged a matinada, an early morning serenade, for one of his holy sweethearts, but the man is a notorious boaster where women are concerned.

*****

20

Serenissima

I quickly accustomed myself to my new life: getting up at dawn to attend to an employer was not unusual. Only the daily gondola trip along the city's green and frequently evil-smelling waterways was new. The beauty of Venice staggered most visitors but, although I admired its glories, I was always aware of its sinister undercurrents.

As the summer advanced the stench from the canals grew more oppressive until a storm came and tides washed the filth of the city out to sea. Gradually, Gaetano explained the complexities of life in this outwardly frivolous but tightly controlled republic. I learned that a metal lion's head set into a wall with an open slit for its mouth signified a place where Venetian citizens could post a letter anonymously denouncing someone to the State.

On one sunny day when we were both free from our duties he took me walking around the city. Our task was to count the lions of Venice; so many stone beasts, but always with wings. This creature was the symbol of the city state. After a short time we had counted so many in one small district that we were forced to give up the task and sit in the sun eating apricots. Afterwards Gaetano told me that I had a beautiful smile.

'But you do not smile often enough.'

Sometimes, we saw the groups of armed ruffianos in the street acting as hired protectors to anyone who could pay for their services. The results of their activities would be quietly disposed of in the canals at dead of night. As the pleasure-mad aristocrats danced all night at balls on the Grand Canal, the secret police garrotted their victims in the dungeons of the Doge's palace. In the notorious prison under the leads of that palace prisoners rotted for years while Venetian laundry women wore satin and furs.

None of these things surprised me. The Spanish rulers in Naples were also cruel and unjust in many ways, but it was the cold, sly cruelty of the Venetian system that chilled me after the chaotic, tempestuous ways of the south. That - and the water, the sinuous, slimy canals that had almost claimed my life and which were the lifelines of this watery paradise. I shuddered if one of the city's huge rats ran over my foot as I stepped out of the gondola. Gaetano laughed and told me that I would soon get used to them. 'The ones on two legs are far worse.'

You must not think that nothing in Venice pleased me. Sometimes, when I had an opportunity to walk alone I loved to look at the little balconies called altanas on the front of the palaces, where grand ladies spread out their hair so that it could be bleached by the sun. Blondes and redheads were the fashion at that time.

Sarah da Costa was as different from Donna Maria as one human being could be from another. Most of the time she seemed to be in a rage but the anger was directed at life itself and her own situation rather than at anyone in particular. The girl chafed at the restrictions placed on her by society, by her father and by her religion. She raged at being confined in the ghetto and longed to travel. Gradually, she confided these things to me while trying to teach me something of the ugly Venetian dialect.

A constant procession of people from all classes and areas of the city came to the da Costa house seeking Jacob's services. The nobility often hired clothes for special occasions and also furniture for the many balls and functions they gave. Jewellery, daggers, fine old paintings and brocades lay about in the rooms, all left as pledges by Venice's pleasure-loving citizens.

'The nobles gamble at the casinos and often lose heavily,' Mistress Sarah explained. 'The poor, of course, always need loans and there is an area around St Barnabas' church where a group of impoverished nobles live. They are called "Barnabotti" and they are good customers,' she laughed. 'They need to keep up appearances.' In addition, Jacob da Costa hired out a gondola to people like Gaetano who plied their trade on the canals. This was forbidden but the authorities looked the other way. He must have come to an arrangement with them.

Only a few days after my arrival in the household I saw the Prince of Venosa and his attendants walk into the da Costa office chamber. I was crossing the hall at the time carrying one of Sarah's elaborate dresses that I held up to cover my face. Nobody glanced my way but the terror that gripped me almost made my heart burst from my breast. The prince did not stay long. When Gaetano collected me that evening he told me that a Neapolitan nobleman had hired his gondola for a few weeks.

'He will pay well,' the young man declared, looking pleased. 'Jacob da Costa recommended me. He is a good man, don't you think, Laura?' I nodded without speaking. I suppose my face must have looked white and drawn. If Gaetano noticed he said nothing, but instead of returning immediately to the house he turned the gondola into a little rio and moored under a humpbacked bridge near the small church of the Miracoli.

'It is the most beautiful church in Venice,' he said, 'and very popular for weddings,' he added, glancing shyly at me. I nodded absently, my mind still on the day's events. Gaetano tugged at my arm. 'Come into the church with me just for a moment. It's wonderful - a miniature paradise.'

Inside the Miracoli we both stared around in delight at this small-scale model of celestial bliss. The delicate traceries, the angels and cherubs that climbed on every column and decorated every screen were captivating, and the glorious coloured ceiling depicting scenes from the life of Christ seemed to be just above our heads.

'This church is not like any other in the city' Gaetano told me. 'It is small and delicate and perfect, bringing heaven closer to earth.' I smiled at him.

'Is that what you tell the visitors you escort here?

'Not always,' he replied seriously, 'only if I think they are sensitive souls who will appreciate the place.'

There was complete silence in the church for a long moment except for the faint lapping of the water only a few feet from the open door. A beam of summer sunshine slanted across the blue and gold interior lighting up the serene Madonna and angels painted on the walls around us. We were kneeling in a pew near the door. I sat perfectly still with my hand almost touching Gaetano's. This is as close to paradise as I will ever be, I thought, as I looked up at the painted ceiling.

For an instant, my mind flew back to the island of Sicily and the golden city of Noto where I had been so happy for a few years. I remembered the Grotto of Demeter and the dozens of small, smiling statuettes lying on the ground, the feeling of peace and well-being there. I suppose it was sinful to be thinking of pagan goddesses while kneeling in the Virgin's miraculous shrine, but I could not help myself.

Later, when we stepped into the gondola and began to drift towards home Gaetano sang me a song that Don Gesualdo had asked him to sing. All the gondoliers in Venice were expected to perform for visitors. He had sung something called "*La Biondina in Gondoleta*" in his pleasing, light tenor voice and the prince had complimented him on his effort.

'I am a singer of fair accomplishment,' he had remarked, 'but I am first and foremost a composer and a musician.' Gaetano commented that the prince 'was most gracious to me.'

I sighed, not wishing to spoil the moment by discussing the real man and his attributes. As we neared the landing stage Gaetano suddenly said, 'I am twenty-eight years old.'

'Are you?' I laughed. 'Do I need to know that?' He looked at me with a serious expression. 'Won't you tell me how old you are, Laura? You have told me very little about yourself.' With good reason, I said silently. I knew that Gaetano was trying to pay court to me in his shy, humorous way and I was flattered, but also alarmed. I was no fit wife for anyone, especially a good man like Gaetano. I had killed a man, I laboured under a curse and I had made a vow of revenge. In addition, I reminded myself mournfully, I was not pretty or special in anyway. I remembered the sight of my face in Donna Maria's mirror all those years ago. And the men had called me *la frigida*.

Gaetano moored the gondola and I made to step out.

'I believe I am twenty seven years old,' I told him, 'perhaps a little less or more. I left my village in Sicily when I had thirteen summers, I think. That was when I entered my lady's service.' I stepped quickly on to the jetty before he could ask me anything else.

There was also the matter of Gaetano's mother who was waiting for us with her usual expression of vinegar when she saw me, an expression that changed to one of adoration as she greeted her son. I knew when I had made an enemy and the signora was definitely an enemy.

'You are late my son, where have you been?'

'I was showing Laura the church of the Miracoli, mother.' The signora gave me a look of pure malice. 'Supper is ready.' She managed to inject a world of meaning into those three words.

My duties in the da Costa household were so light that Sire da Costa sometimes asked me to accompany him to auctions on the Rialto where debtors' clothes and other items were sold. Occasionally, Mistress Sarah would come too, heavily veiled, in order to choose fabric for her latest gown

The flow of people into the da Costa house with possessions to pledge or redeem continued daily but I never again saw the prince cross the threshold. I knew that he was due to leave the city and continue on to Ferrara but my only source of information was Gaetano who would tell me where he had taken the prince that day. I had explained my connection with him, knowing that he would not betray my confidence to anyone.

'He has visited the composer Gabrieli several times and often listens to the music in St Mark's.' I also learned about the banquet at the Arsenal, but that scandal was common knowledge throughout the city. Mistress Sarah had heard it from Isaac, the hunchback in the ghetto. The city had given a banquet in the prince's honour, as was the custom with visiting dignitaries. The guest had found the music not to his liking and the singers of poor quality. He had left the hall in disgust while speeches of welcome were being made. This had caused outrage and it was thought that the arrogant visitor would be leaving Venice very soon. I knew that such behaviour was not unusual but it usually happened in private rather than at state banquets.

As I grew accustomed to my new life in Venice, split between the da Costa house in the ghetto and the Giovanelli family, I realised that I felt happier than at any time since my days in Noto. True, I would have sudden pangs of sorrow and moments of piercing guilt, but these came at unexpected moments. Most of the time I was content…no, more than content.

I had not expected to feel this way again. I was a fallen creature, stained with blood, a witness to slaughter and a killer in my own right. I wondered in my heart if I had ever been innocent. My birth had caused my mother's death and the peddler had despoiled me when I was little more than a child.

But Gaetano was falling in love with me. I knew this as a woman always knows these things. The looks he gave me, the little gestures, his way of brushing his hand against my cheek or my hair accidentally, and the daily journey to the ghetto in the gondola told me the truth. This, in particular, filled his mother with fury.

'You are wasting time, my son, losing good money. She can walk well enough.' This would be said with a malevolent look in my direction. Gaetano ignored her and those journeys were precious times away from her hawk-like gaze.

Her hatred almost scalded me when I came near her. Was it because I was a foreigner, not a Venetian? Or was it because she wanted to keep her son for herself? I could see that she did not understand why he was attracted to me and, indeed, I could not understand it either. I did not waste time thinking of these things. I simply basked in the feeling of pleasure. I knew it would last only until I told the full truth about myself. Then Gaetano would surely recoil in horror and my short idyll would be over.

21

Sarah

My time with Mistress Sarah in the ghetto also gave me pleasure. Her father always treated me kindly and his daughter soon accepted me. I think she was glad to have a confidante in the house, even one like me. She persevered in teaching me the Venetian dialect and explained daily life in that small but extraordinary quarter of Venice. She was a creature of moods: I sensed her frustration with her life. It would come boiling out of her in rages that were soon over and often followed by simmering silences.

I can see her now, lying on her stomach in bed, clutching one of her grand dresses, with the bed curtains pulled tight. When I opened them a little to offer some soothing chamomile tea she shrieked at me, 'Go away! Leave me alone; I want nothing.' I closed the curtains. A moment later she opened them a crack, 'fetch me some candied figs, my shawl and my red velvet slippers.' Then she would drink the tea and return meekly to her father's accounts.

In quiet moments when she read a book beside the window Mistress Sarah would look up and gaze out over the bustling square below and begin to speak about her troubles. One day she threw the book down and exclaimed, 'let us go for a walk; it's too nice a day to be shut up here like chickens in a coop.'

She swept down the stairs taking advantage of her father's meeting with the synagogue elders. I knew it was my mistress's responsibility to oversee the kitchen and choose the menus but she preferred to leave everything to Rachel, the elderly cook who had been her childhood nurse.

At the door of the house I helped her to put on her highest zoccoli- the ones with mother of pearl inlay. She staggered around the square keeping close to the houses, as propriety demanded. I followed a few paces behind. A few of the older Jewish matrons in the street clucked disapprovingly at the length of her train and the amount of lace on her gown, but she ignored them all. As we walked by the canal lifting our faces to the sun she suddenly swung around and faced me for a moment.

'My father wishes me to be married, you know. He fears I am already too old at nineteen to be of interest to a suitable husband. ' I tried to put on a sympathetic expression but my mistress noticed nothing as she turned again and addressed her words to the dark waters of the canal and a family of ducks riding the in the wake of a gondola.

'I do not want to be married, I want to live! I want to leave this ghetto and see the world. I cannot even do the things that Christian girls do in Venice and they do little enough. Why was I born female? I know I could run my father's business as well as he does, but he allows me to be nothing more than his secretary.' I leaned against a stone plinth watching as the young woman wailed her anguish into the water.

'Prayers and good works, modest dress and the care of children, that is the life for a good Jewish girl. I want something different, I want…I want-not this.' She waved her hand at the towering tenements behind her and the people scurrying across the square on various errands.

I patted her arm gently, 'perhaps the right husband would help you to do some of these things?' I suggested. 'If you married a man from another city or country you would be able to travel.' She shrugged and fell silent.

As we walked back to the house I began to describe the golden city of Noto, hesitantly at first, as I tried to convey the beauty of the place. My mistress listened avidly for a moment then interrupted.

'Venice is also a beautiful city, many say it is the most beautiful of all, but what does that matter if you have no freedom?' I said nothing; I wanted to point out that freedom to move around went hand in hand with freedom to starve if you were poor.

'Why am I like this?' the young woman whispered. 'I do not mean to be wicked, may the Everlasting One be my witness.' She gave a dry sob and stumbled as she tried to rush the last few yards to the house. I hurried after her feeling the weight of the young woman's sorrow that re-awakened my own ghosts.

As soon as we entered the house Rachel appeared with her hands covered in flour.

'Come, come!' she cried 'what are you thinking of, child?' She lapsed into their own language but I knew what she was saying. Her workload was heavy, there was a feast day approaching and Mistress Sarah was neglecting her responsibilities. Without a word the young woman threw a covering over her finery and began furiously peeling and chopping vegetables for the soup.

'Take these,' she muttered, kicking the zoccoli in my direction. Then Rachel waved me away fearing that my presence would contaminate her kosher kitchen.

As I left the house I came upon a young man, finely dressed, loitering in the entrance hall waiting to see the master. He asked me to fetch Sire da Costa because he wanted to pawn his hat medallion.

'It is a handsome piece,' I ventured, gazing at the figure of a saint on horseback, chased in silver against a background of beaten copper edged in gold. The young man shrugged as I laid the medallion on a bench. 'St George isn't fashionable anymore.'

In my quiet moments I wondered about the prince. I knew he was now in Ferrara and married to the unfortunate Leonora d'Este, while I was dallying in Venice, drifting away from my solemn vow, seeking my own happiness. I thought of Gaetano and his shy courtship of me. Guilt flooded through me and my cheeks burned.

I knew that Gesualdo would return to Venice on his journey back to the south. Another chance would present itself. But in the night, I would lie awake facing my own cowardice, my lack of will. It was simply that I did not want to die. Here in the water city I had found a measure of contentment. Someone cared for me – such a wonderful thing had never happened to me before. I had found a reason to live for the first time since Donna Maria's death.

Also, I knew that I could never kill anyone in cold blood, not even Gesualdo. I had poisoned Aldo Pretti in a fit of rage but I could not approach anyone like a thief in the night. I would push these thoughts away as I waited in the red and gold Venetian sunset for the soft swish of Gaetano's gondola.

22

Extracts from the
Journal of Carlo Gesualdo.

June 20.1594

    These past few weeks since my arrival in Ferrara and the marriage with Leonora have been the most splendid of my life.

    The reception given to me on my arrival and after the marriage has been most generous. I found the city decorated with triumphal arches and hung with all manner of decorations.

    The Duke was graciously pleased to arrange all manner of musical entertainments, ballets and masques as well as a military display. Fountains ran with wine and Leonora was much occupied in throwing coins to the poor. We also heard the nuns of San Vito whose singing and playing are unrivalled in this country.

    The Duke keeps a vast number of musicians who play on every conceivable instrument. The Duchess Margherita herself has in her service a concerto di donne, three young women who sing like angels and play upon the harp and the lute. Every night they perform for two hours before the court and the ladies go about with the Duchess in her carriage.

Baldini's press in Ferrara will shortly print my book of madrigals. Leonora does well enough as a wife.

July 2

Today I leave Ferrara to begin the journey home to Gesualdo. I leave the city with a heavy heart but business affairs call me back for a few months. Leonora will remain here. At least I can look forward to another stay in Venice where I hope to meet Gabrieli again and sample the musical delights of San Marco. Any gentleman would wish to spend time in the Serenissima whenever possible. I shall also visit Bardi in Florence. I have heard that he has devised a new musical entertainment called simply opera.

23

A Proposal

We were back in the church of the Miracoli one early August day when Gaetano finally plucked up the courage to ask me to marry him. He was always finding excuses to linger on the journey home in the evening and I seldom objected. Often, he would propel the gondola down unknown small canals to show me yet another of the wonders of his city, but the Miracoli remained our favourite place.

He turned to me as we sat at the back of the church gazing at the painted ceiling once again and took my hand.

'Do you think you could be happy here in Venice, Laura?'

'Of course.' I laughed, choosing to misunderstand him. 'I am happy. Why should I not be happy? I have good employment and friends here.' His face remained very serious.

'I meant could you be happy here with me - as my wife?' My moment of truth had arrived. Now I would have to tell him everything.

'I am too old for you,' I said, still unable to tell him the truth. He squeezed my hand hard until I squealed. 'Stop being silly and give me an answer!'

'When you know my story, Gaetano, you will not want to marry me.' He shook his head. 'Whatever you say, it will make no difference.'

Once again, there was nothing but a liquid silence in the church. A beam of spring sunshine slanted across the high altar.

Then it all came tumbling out: the whole dark, sadistic tale of Sicilian sorrow and Neapolitan madness. I spared him nothing. 'So, you see, I cannot be a wife to anyone. I am a damned soul.' He was silent for a moment and then he squeezed my hand again, gently, this time.

'It is a sorry tale but such things happen here too. I would probably have done the same for my friends. You can receive absolution, Laura, if you confess. We could be married here in the Miracoli.' Poor Gaetano; he was still trying to concoct a fairy tale ending for my terrible story.

'How can I receive absolution? I'm not sorry for what I did. I would do it again – and I probably will. Remember, I made a vow to avenge my mistress.' Gaetano shook his head; 'Did you promise to defend her and avenge her while she was still alive?'

I nodded, 'I swore a solemn oath in Sicily and I renewed it at her tomb.' He grasped my hands in his own. 'I don't think you had any right to make that vow, Laura, and I don't think your lady would have expected you to do such a thing. You cannot kill a prince. Enough of these murderous fantasies…marry me and be happy in Venice.'

And, of course, I agreed: part of me desperately wanted to be normal, to be cherished and loved. The dark half was still there but I chose to ignore it at that time. We sat for a long time, close together on the wooden seat, his arm around my shoulder, our heads close together. An understanding had been reached and sealed with a kiss. As we stepped into the gondola and began to drift towards home Gaetano sang to me again.

As we neared the house he grinned his infectious grin and said, 'I don't think you should tell your story to my mother, Laura. She will not take it well.' That was certainly true. When her son told her of our intended marriage, the signora appeared to have a fit. If she could have spat blood she would have covered the walls with her own life essence. I quietly finished preparing the meal the old woman had abandoned while Gaetano attempted to calm her. She refused to eat with us and huddled in a corner where she sat with her shawl over her head, rocking and moaning as if in mourning. Gaetano shrugged and grimaced at me.

'She will accept things after a time; she has no choice.' I doubted that. The signora would always be my enemy. I knew these things. I was from Sicily.

Later, Gaetano poured some wine and urged his mother to drink our health, 'If you love me.' She accepted the glass reluctantly. Her only comment was, 'She is a foreigner, a nobody. She is too old and she has no dowry.' At that I rose and went to my bundle of belongings. I removed a small velvet pouch and took something from it. At the table I placed one of Donna Maria's pearls in front of my future mother-in-law.

'This is my dowry. It was given to me by my lady. I do not come empty handed.'

The old woman's eyes bulged slightly as she stared at the jewel but Gaetano picked it up and placed it in my hand.

'I know how much it means to you. Keep it for now. Later, we shall see.' His mother screamed and jumped to her feet.

'Of course, we need it now! We are poor. Why are you such a fool my son?' I said nothing but I replaced the pearls in their pouch in my bosom for safe keeping.

When I returned to the ghetto on the following day the atmosphere was strained. I found my young mistress sunk in despair behind tightly drawn bed curtains. Eventually, she emerged, white faced, to announce that her father had told her last night that a husband had been found for her.

'Shmuel the matchmaker arranged it all. He is a businessman, aged forty -five, from the Jewish community on the island of Cyprus.' So, she would travel away from Venice after all. 'He will arrive in Venice in three months.' Her voice was expressionless. 'We will be married here and I will return with him. The dowry has been agreed and I must prepare my trousseau.' She flung her arms out and cried, 'We will not speak of it again. There is nothing to be done.'

Later, when her mood had lifted a little I told her of my own intended marriage.

'Is it a love match, Laura?'

'Yes...yes, it is.' I replied hearing the wonder in my voice. She smiled and said, 'you must marry soon so that I can watch your wedding before I leave.' I grew hot with embarrassment.

'I don't think that will be possible, madam. The ceremony has been arranged for Saturday in two weeks' time.' That would be the Jewish Sabbath. How could Mistress Sarah escape from the ghetto to watch a Christian ceremony when she would be in the synagogue, closely watched by her father?

'I will find a way, but I shall need your help. You must bring me some boy's clothes. Perhaps I shall cut off my hair to aid the disguise.' She gave me an impish smile. I was aghast. 'What would your father say? You are about to be married.'

'Perhaps the bridegroom will cancel the contract,' she laughed. 'Didn't you know that a Jewish woman is required to shave her head when she marries and to wear false hair?' I shook my head wondering why there were so many rules and commandments for women and so few for men.

I was afraid of angering my master. Jacob da Costa had been good to me – and to Gaetano, and now I was being asked to help his madcap daughter to offend him in a particularly outrageous way. I quailed at the thought. When I told Gaetano he almost toppled out of the gondola.

24

Lilies for Farewells

'She is a crazy woman! We could all be executed for such an act. You must refuse to help her.' I shrugged; 'You do not know her. When she is determined nothing will stop her.'

Mistress Sarah had seized on my marriage as something to relieve her misery and boredom. She redoubled her attempts to improve my Venetian dialect and threw open her closet to find a gown for me. She decided to watch the wedding from a gondola near the Miracoli church. At least she had not asked to enter the church.

'I think my yellow brocade would be very suitable for you. I hardly ever wear it. You could wear a white silk underskirt and you will need a length of white lace for a veil. I am sure my father would give you some as a gift.' I thanked her while thinking that yellow did not suit me at all. I looked longingly at a grass green silk gown and then remembered the signora's words. 'She is a nobody, and she is too old.'

On Friday morning, the day before the wedding, Mistress Sarah made herself look as sickly as possible, smearing her face with cream and white powder and hiding behind the bed curtains.

'Is she feverish?' her father asked me anxiously, fearful for his only child. I tried to give a nod and a gesture that could have meant anything. Later, when the Sabbath arrived he went off to his devotions having instructed Rachel to send for a doctor. Herbal teas were passed up from the kitchen and Mistress Sarah insisted that she did not need a doctor's attentions.

As soon as we were alone we tried on clothes in desperate haste. Mistress Sarah dressed herself in her boy's costume and I put on the yellow brocade gown. I attempted to tame my unruly curls once more but I refused her suggestion of covering the mole on my face with a patch. Such affectations were not for servants.

'You will need something to wear with the gown; try these shoes.' I obediently removed my boots and tried to force my sturdy peasant feet into some tiny, red-heeled slippers without success. Then Mistress Sarah changed back into her normal clothes and I re-arranged her auburn hair into the two horns on the forehead, Venetian style. I had realized that my mistress was not a natural red head. She followed the fashions enthusiastically, applying henna to her hair and sitting in the sun to obtain the coveted red-gold hue.

As the day drew on I grew sick in my stomach with nerves while my mistress grew more excited. 'I shall be out of the ghetto for an hour or two and no-one will know who I am. Can you imagine that, Laura?' Her eyes shone in the grotesque white mask she had painted on. Her own forthcoming marriage was never mentioned.

I left the house as dusk was falling, clutching the yellow gown and its white underskirt. The master had returned and he called out a blessing on my marriage as I walked away. Rachel had made a box of sweetmeats as a gift. Mistress Sarah's white face appeared for a second at an upper window. She waved and was gone.

Gaetano was waiting impatiently in the moored gondola as I walked across the bridge carrying the gown. He clutched me in a tight embrace before I sank down on the seat with the folds of the yellow dress billowing around me.

'It is a fine gown,' he remarked, 'but we could have bought something new for you.' I smiled and squeezed his hand, knowing how little money he had and imagining his mother's reaction.

'This is richer than anything we could afford. It was very kind of Mistress Sarah to lend it to me.' Later that night, as Gaetano celebrated with his fellow gondoliers, my future mother-in-law watched as I boiled artichoke root in wine and drank a full beaker. This potion, according to Sister Antony, was guaranteed to lessen the rank smell of the armpits.

Later that evening I slipped into a church to make the obligatory confession before the nuptial mass. I did not go to the Miracoli or my mother-in-law's church, San Geremia. I deliberately chose a place where I was unknown.

I could not tell the priest that I had killed someone in Naples. I knew that I would not be given absolution. I made an act of contrition and begged Christ to forgive me. May His Mother and all the saints intercede for me. I knew I was a hypocrite but I had made a vow and nothing could alter that.

The wedding day dawned fine and sunny with a chorus of Venice's elegant cats serenading me from the rooftops when I opened the window. I felt too nervous to eat and when I dressed in my borrowed finery Signora Giovanelli looked me up and down and pronounced the colour all wrong.

'You are too sallow, too southern to wear yellow,' she said with evident satisfaction. Under her breath she muttered, 'and too old,' knowing I would hear. I turned away remembering the glimpse of my face in Donna Maria's mirror, the wiry black curls, the mole under my eye, the tooth that was beginning to blacken. I resolved to keep my mouth closed as much as possible.

When Gaetano appeared, he looked more handsome than ever in his velvet cape edged with silver thread. He presented me with a sheaf of flowers, orange blossom entwined with jasmine. I buried my face in the scented blossoms and then looked up at him.

'Why do you want to marry me, my love?' He picked up the lace veil and draped it over my head.

'Who knows? Because you are so contrary, probably! ' We stepped in to the gondola, rowed by our neighbour, Federico.

The nuptial mass was celebrated in front of a handful of Gaetano's neighbours and friends who, if they wondered why he had chosen this sallow-skinned foreigner, were too polite to comment. His mother sat at the back of the church with a veil over her face, telling her rosary beads in a loud whisper. The perfume of orange blossom was in my nose as Gaetano placed the ring on my finger and I experienced a moment of pure joy.

As we left the dazzling sunlit splendour of the Miracoli and stepped into an equally dazzling Venetian midday, the angelus bell began to chime and I shaded my eyes, anxiously searching for a glimpse of Mistress Sarah. From under the small, humpbacked bridge the prow of a gondola peeked out followed by the head and shoulders of a "boy" wearing a velvet cap. The "boy" waved frantically to us, laughing and blowing kisses. I would always remember her like that in years to come. As the gondola passed by I tried to throw the flowers to her but they fell into the water and floated under the bridge.

25

Silk

We were heading for Burano, one of the islands in the lagoon where a friend had offered us a room for the night. Considerate as always, Gaetano had known that I would not have wanted to spend our wedding night with my mother-in-law nearby. We would have a few hours alone together before returning to our work the following morning.

On the small island with its brightly painted houses and fishermen's boats our friends drank to our health and everyone ate a festive meal of mussel soup, pasticcio of polenta and delicious cherries brought from Treviso as a gift for us.

I changed out of the yellow brocade and gave it to my mother-in-law to take back to Venice. The signora barely spoke during the meal and when questioned said she felt unwell. She obliged us all by being taken home early.

In our gondola, we floated quietly back to the city in the dawn light when the lagoon shimmered in the pearly haze that drew so many artists to this place. Little wavelets came and went almost unnoticed - a strange, rippling effect of the water that I had never seen before. Gaetano told me that in the city the light reflected the ripples onto the ceiling - an effect local people called "la vecchia," referring to the lines on an old woman's face.

We said little; listening to the soft swish of the water and the crying of the sea birds. The first night together had passed. Gaetano seemed happy enough. He was considerate and gentle but I knew that what had happened to me in my youth prevented me from fully enjoying the act of love. Did men expect that from their wives? I did not know. The priests spoke only of Christian duty for women. There were twenty thousand prostitutes in Venice who supplied what was lacking in the marriage bed.

Gaetano was not like that. He was loyal and loving. I remembered with a glowing heart how he stroked my face gently before he helped me take off my brocade gown.

'You do not need finery, my love,' he said. 'You are enough for me.' As we lay in each other's arms and joined our bodies together I knew that he would always be faithful to me and I would always love him.

When we arrived home Signora Giovanelli told us that a boy had come from the da Costa house to say that my services were not required that day. I knew then that Mistress Sarah's expedition had been discovered. Gaetano returned to his work and I tidied my clothes. When I folded the yellow brocade gown I realized that the white underskirt was missing. The signora had brought the clothes back to Venice.

I said nothing when my mother-in-law told me that she

was going out for a while. She gave me a furtive look, picked up her basket and drew her shawl over her head. Curiosity overcame me and I decided to follow her. Her behaviour was always so odd - and what did she want with the underskirt? I was convinced that she had stolen it.

The signora passed quickly into the maze of alleyways that she knew so well and I followed at a distance shielded by the throng of people. Some of the alleyways were so narrow that two people could scarcely pass each other. The Venetians called them linings.

My mother-in-law hurried down the Street of the Assassins and knocked on a door in a dark courtyard. Unable to follow, I stopped a passer- by and asked if he knew who lived in the house. The man spat on the cobbles and told me that Gabriella Forri lived there.

'She is a witch and should be drowned in the lagoon.' He spat at my feet again and walked away. A woman emerged from the nearby bakery and saw me looking up at the house.

'Women and girls go there for love potions – and other things…' she muttered before hurrying away. I leaned against a wall imagining what my mother-in-law would be saying to the witch.

'My son has married a bitch from the South who will bring us all to grief. You must help me to get rid of her.'

There was nothing I could do but return to the house. Later, I asked one of our neighbours about Gabriella Forri. Thinking that I wanted a charm to keep my husband faithful, the neighbour laughed and explained that an article of clothing used by the man would be needed for the spell to work.

'And what if the intention was evil?' I asked.

'Well,' the woman replied, 'the witch would need an article of clothing or something that had the person's bodily fluids smeared on it – perhaps menstrual blood in the case of a woman.' I went back to the house thoughtfully. It would be easy for my mother-in-law to obtain such a thing. I looked up at the high window of our room and saw the

signora looking down at me. She made the sign of the cross and moved away.

I continued to fret inwardly about the disappearance of Sarah's underskirt but I controlled my feelings whenever my mother-in-law was around and I decided not to mention anything to Gaetano. Men were not interested in such matters.

Mistress Sarah also was completely unconcerned when I returned the yellow brocade gown and admitted the loss of its undergarment. The young woman just shrugged and forgot the incident. She was still excited about her expedition to watch the wedding. Her father, as usual, had punished her only a little. Perhaps he accepted that her opportunities for such small adventures would soon be over.

As the weeks passed the da Costa household became obsessed with the imminent marriage. Preparations were already in hand: Rachel had complained loudly to anyone who would listen that she could not cope alone in the kitchen. Eventually, Sire da Costa weakened and hired a young lad as her assistant, as well as another maid.

My main task was to re-organize yet again my mistress's vast wardrobe. Gowns that were unsuitable for a Jewish matron were discarded and several of them were given to me. Gaetano said I looked like a duchess in my second-hand velvets and silks. 'Except for her colouring,' sniffed his mother.

My mistress kept a piece of paper torn from one of her father's ledgers on which she marked off the days and weeks until the arrival of her prospective bridegroom. The paper was kept under her pillow. I watched, saddened by the girl's despair but unable to help.

26

An Arrangement

Once or twice she spoke of girls who had run away from the ghetto. A few had married Christians and were lost forever to their people. Others had vanished without trace. At least one had drowned herself after her lover had tired of her.

'She had no dowry,' said Sarah quietly. 'Christians think we are all rich. A wealthy Jewess is sometimes acceptable as a wife, if she converts, but never a poor one.' We both knew that running away was not an option in her case. She had no lover or protector outside the ghetto and she loved her father too much to cause him grief.

With the arrival of November with its mists and rain and high water we spent much of the time in the lofty bedchamber looking out over the square. Mistress Sarah described the Jewish marriage ceremony, the breaking of the wine glass that symbolized the destruction of the Temple in Jerusalem; the canopy under which the bride and groom stood that represented a tent from their time in the desert. Sometimes she read aloud from the popular romances that Venetians love and which she smuggled into the house with my help.

She was surprised when I told her that I could write my name and even read a few words, having been taught by Gaetano.

'And how did he learn?' she asked.

'The priest taught him: his mother wanted him to take holy orders but he followed his father and became a gondolier.'

'It is a good calling,' she remarked. 'Gondoliers are highly valued in this city. You will never go hungry, Laura, yourself or your child.' We both looked down at my thin body, which gave nothing away. Only the bouts of sickness and fatigue revealed that I was pregnant.

'How does it feel?' Mistress Sarah asked curiously. 'What is it like to have life inside you?'

'It feels…strange,' I replied slowly, 'there is a kind of heaviness…it's difficult to describe.'

Gaetano had been delighted with the news but his mother's sharp features had contracted even more. She watched me at all times with a hostile stare. I ate at the da Costa house as far as possible and made the food myself when I was at home. After the incident of the witch and the underskirt I was convinced that the signora meant to harm me in some way. Poison would be a convenient choice. I was in a position to know that.

At last, November drew to a close and my master announced that the ship bringing the bridegroom, whose name was Salomon, was expected hourly. On the day he arrived, the master went to meet him with Shmuel the marriage broker, and another man who was Mistress Sarah's uncle.

She had been told to dress suitably and I had laid out a high-necked, dark blue gown with a modest veil and a short train. Tiny pearl earrings had replaced the ostentatious jewellery she loved. Her father nodded approvingly as he left.

As soon as the men left the square my mistress raced upstairs, telling me to follow her. With a last gesture of rebellion, she ordered me to help her on with the flamboyant emerald velvet gown edged with gold lace that she had worn when I first saw her. The same rows of large pearls were added together with gold slippers. She arranged herself in the dining chamber with her skirts billowing around her and her auburn hair flowing loose in the sea of green. Her expression was one of passionate defiance.

Rachel wept and wrung her hands. I tried to persuade her to change but the girl would not be moved. She sat white-faced and silent until the men arrived. I cracked open the door of the chamber just wide enough to peer in.

I saw six men. Salomon had travelled with two older relatives. They stood on the threshold of the dining hall and there was a long silence. The expression on the master's face was terrifying. For once, he was pale with fury, rendered speechless. The bridegroom was similarly struck dumb.

He was a short, but quite handsome man, with a well-kept beard and dark, expressive eyes. Those eyes were staring at his fiancée in shocked admiration. At length, he turned and blurted something to his companions in a language I could not understand. It might have been Greek or Hebrew. Then he turned to Mistress Sarah and spoke in halting Italian, telling her how beautiful she was.

'I am a fortunate man,' he said to her father who bowed and gave a strained smile. I wished I could see the expression on my mistress's face which was turned away in shadow. A few moments later she returned to her chamber. I slipped away before the celebration supper began. The delicious smells of roasting chicken and tagliatelle followed me along the street. Rachel always cooked this dish with sultanas and pine nuts.

During the few days that remained before the wedding there was little time for conversation. Mistress Sarah became increasingly pale and silent. My remarks about the groom's good looks went unanswered. The piece of paper under the pillow was crumpled and tossed aside.

Naturally, I was not invited to the wedding ceremony. I helped to dress the bride and waved her off as she was escorted to the nearby synagogue. A large crowd of neighbours and friends followed to honour the da Costa family. As she made the circuit of the square cries and shouts of joy rang out.

'What will I do now?' I asked Gaetano. 'My mistress is leaving; I shall need a new position.'

'We shall see,' he replied. 'Soon you will have a baby to care for. Perhaps you should stay at home?' I considered this suggestion and disliked it. I could not stay all day with my mother-in-law and neither would I leave my child with that woman.

There remained only the final farewells. I hugged my employer who had become a friend in a few short months. I whispered that I was sure everything would go well, that ginger was a fine remedy for sea-sickness, that the groom seemed like a good man.

Mistress Sarah just nodded. 'What can I do?' she said softly, 'It is too late.'

With a final backward look the party embarked on several gondolas on a last journey down the Grand Canal to the waiting ship. I returned home feeling sick in my stomach and sick at heart.

It grew colder as the year drew to a close. Once or twice I called at the da Costa house to ask for news of Mistress Sarah. Had the ship arrived in Cyprus?

'It is too soon,' said Sire da Costa, 'we must wait for messengers to return to Venice.'

Christmas came and went with a grand procession of the Patriarch to St Mark's for the mass of the Nativity. Venetians celebrated, as always, with wine and feasting although Carnival was only two months away. I felt better physically as the pregnancy advanced but I was still full of anxiety for Mistress Sarah, a dread that I could not explain.

The New Year was well under way when the news came. I found the master huddled in a chair in his study, his clothes awry, his beard uncombed. Rachel had taken to her bed and was gravely ill.

'She cannot be dead.' I cried. 'Please tell me that Mistress Sarah is not dead.'

He raised his head. 'The ship was captured by the Turks. The men were killed and my daughter was taken prisoner. I believe she has been sold into the Sultan's harem.' His voice broke and he beat his chest. 'May the Eternal One forgive me, it would be better if she had been killed.'

As I left the silent, unlit house I thought I heard Mistress Sarah's voice whispering in the shadows, 'I only wanted to be free.'

27

Extract from the Journal of
Carlo Gesualdo, Prince of Venosa

Dec. 8.1594

I have returned again to Ferrara after my business in Gesualdo. Leonora and I have taken up residence in the Palace of Marco de Pio.

My musical activities here give me the greatest pleasure. I play and compose daily and I have had the opportunity to hear the extraordinary archicembalo played by the court organist Luzzasco Luzzaschi. This instrument is a two-manual microtonal harpsichord which plays in any key with equal temperament. It was invented by Nicolo Vicentino and is surely a marvel. Luzzaschi's chromatic harmonies are admirable and they have given me new inspiration for my own compositions,

I am only truly happy when composing and playing. When I am about the daily business of life I have only to close my eyes and I can see the fiery glow of the candles on my harpsichord. I smell the sharp smell of ink and hear the scratching of my pen as I write my compositions. I must arrange a sala de cembalo at the castle when I return to Gesualdo.

I have visited the Duke's music room at the Palazzo Diamanti where I found an amazing variety of instruments being played by numerous musicians. I spent several hours examining many printed books of music and manuscripts. It is a source of pride to me that my compositions will be printed here by Vittorio Baldini at the ducal press, joining this illustrious company.

The English composer John Dowland paid a short visit to the court recently and I enjoyed hearing his compositions. He is of a melancholy disposition and his work reflects this. In particular, his collection of twenty-one pieces for viol, consort and lute called Lachrimae. His pavane Semper Dowland, Semper Dolens exactly matches my own mood and personality. I look forward to playing some of his compositions in my own music room.

It is said he is a secret Catholic, fomenting plots against the heretic Queen Elizabeth, but, naturally, he vigorously denies this. In my opinion, he is too cowardly to indulge in such dangerous pursuits. He is of a nervous nature more suited to the lute than the halberd, according to gossip at the court.

In the evenings, I avail myself of the pleasures of the city. The whores of Ferrara are almost as good as those of Venice, and somewhat cheaper. As for the noble ladies of the city, some have proved more than willing.

Leonora bores me, as I have frequently told her. She is given to weeping and wringing her hands at such times but I do not stay to witness her tantrums. Yesterday I had occasion to beat her when she interrupted me during the last passage of my composition, ardo il mio cor. My fury knew no bounds but I was careful not to mark her. We dine with the Duke tonight.

I am not sure of the Duke's disposition regarding wives. It is rumoured that he disposed of his first wife Lucrezia de Medici because of her wanton behaviour. If true, then I would expect a degree of sympathy from him, but it is, of course, a matter of family honour.

The present Duchess, the Serenissima Margherita Gonzaga d'Este, is a great patron of the arts and shares her husband's love of music. In this, at least, they are compatible, even though not one of his three wives have produced an heir.

Leonora has no great interest in my musical accomplishments although she enjoys the music of the court; hence my boredom.

I have received word from the poet Tasso who now resides in Naples. He is out of favour with the Duke here in Ferrara. He begs me to intercede on his behalf. To this end he has sent a poem in praise of my new marriage bound in a book in white leather with gilt edgings. I showed the poem to Leonora telling her that Tasso was much admired by my first wife, Donna Maria. Several expressions passed swiftly across her face at my words.

*****

28

"Many Waters Cannot Quench Love"

That winter in Venice seemed endless to me. I dragged myself through my everyday life and its daily duties as if I carried all the sorrows of the world as well as the burden of pregnancy. Looking back, I remember those months only for the darkness and the chill mists. All the sounds of Venice became sinister, the crying of the cats resembled the wailing of abandoned infants and the screams of revellers during carnival sounded like the shrieks of the damned.

The smells of the city also grew sharper; the overpowering odour of rotting fish, once simply unpleasant, now made me retch. The dank, sweet smell of the canals and the perfume of roasting coffee -the devil's beverage - were equally horrible. I wondered whether this new sensitivity to sounds and smells was the result of pregnancy or simply due to my sadness about Mistress Sarah. I had added more weight to the sack of guilt and grief I carried with me.

I could tell that Gaetano was worried about me. We had grown very close during the months since our wedding. Already we had reached the point where we could signal our feelings to each other without words. This was often necessary when Signora Giovanelli was around.

Now that I was no longer a maidservant I had no excuse to leave the room we shared with my mother-in-law. It was important to find a new way to make some money. With another pair of hands at home Gaetano's mother decided to take in extra laundry and she made it clear that I was to assist her with this as much as possible.

After the news about my mistress I made only one more trip into the ghetto to see Sire da Costa. I knew that the prayers for the dead had been said for Mistress Sarah and that left a cold feeling in my heart. Even if we would never see her again it seemed such a final gesture. Rachel, her old nurse, had died only weeks after the news had reached them and Sire da Costa was preparing to leave Venice.

Since the disappearance of his daughter the old man had lost interest in everything - in his work, in food, in life generally. He planned to travel to Rome where he had some distant relatives.

'Perhaps I shall start afresh,' he told me without much conviction. Physically, he had shrunk in the last few months. Standing next to me with my swollen belly he looked like a stooped, wrinkled child, his velvet, fur-trimmed clothes hanging loosely on his shrivelled frame.

'I have something to give you before you leave' he said. He went upstairs and returned with a bundle - the yellow brocade dress I had worn for my wedding.

'I know my daughter would have wanted you to keep it...to remember her by.' His voice shook a little as he handed me the package wrapped carefully in a piece of silk.

I took it unwillingly, trying not to sound insincere as I thanked him. I had always disliked the dress for its colour and now it would be a permanent reminder of my mistress's fate. Tears poured down my face as I turned away from the house knowing I would never see the master again. He raised his hand in a blessing. 'May the Eternal One keep you and your child from all harm.' He closed the door gently.

The package remained unopened until Gaetano returned that evening. After we had eaten I showed it to him and he exclaimed, 'Isn't that your wedding dress?'

'It was never mine,' I reminded him, 'it was Mistress Sarah's dress - and the underskirt also.'

'I hope no bad luck will come with it, especially now.' Gaetano looked anxiously at my growing belly. His mother made a curious little noise in her throat. When I looked at her she had turned as white as my wedding veil. I stared at her suspiciously saying, 'the underskirt was lost so I could never wear the dress again.'

'Are you feeling unwell, mother?' Gaetano said as his mother continued to make sounds like a trapped bird. The old woman shook her head and resumed sewing by the window.

During Carnival Gaetano had been busier than ever as the Venetians danced and feasted, gambled and lusted all over the city. A gondola was a favourite place for an assignation with a lover, another man's wife or whoever took one's fancy. He was paid well to find a mooring in a quiet little canal or to make a long trip into the loneliness of the lagoon.

Often, he would try to entertain us with stories of his famous and infamous clients, the suicidal gamblers he had saved after they had lost everything at the casino, the incriminating articles of clothing left behind in the gondola.

Sometimes he would succeed in making me laugh and the heaviness would lift for a while. Then we would talk about the child, discuss names and talk of the future, as parents will.

'If it is a boy he will follow in my footsteps' said Gaetano. 'One day I shall have my own gondola. He will be a fortunate young man.'

'You could have your own vessel now if you used your wife's jewels,' his mother remarked, shooting a venomous look in my direction. I ignored her bile, having already decided that I would give my husband the second pearl.

I smiled at him, 'What if the child is a girl?' The signora muttered something inaudible under her breath and Gaetano laughed.

'A girl will need the pearls so that she can make a good marriage.' His mother snorted.

The news of the capture of the Venetian ship on which Mistress Sarah had sailed had been received with fury by the City authorities. It was rumoured that plans were afoot to seek revenge, or at least to demand reparations from the Turks. Sometimes prisoners in the hands of the infidel could be ransomed but if a woman was sold into the Sultan's harem it would be impossible to obtain her release, even though the Jews were generally on better terms with the Turks than the Christians. Sire da Costa had told me that.

There was little news of the prince at this time, although Gaetano took the trouble to enquire of travellers coming from Ferrara. He would do anything to please me.

One day he took the composer Gabrieli from St Mark's to the Madonna del Horto and during the trip he asked the maestro if he had had heard anything regarding the musical prince. Gabrieli remarked that Don Gesualdo had published a number of books of madrigals in Ferrara and also at Venice.

'I hear his music is received with astonishment at the Duke's court,' the composer added drily; 'as it well might be.'

I laughed when I heard this. 'You have not heard those compositions,' I told my husband. 'You have not suffered as I have.' I remembered how my mistress, Donna Maria, had tried to block those sounds from her ears.

By the end of March spring was peering over the distant mountains and occasionally spending a day in the water city. Blue skies and uncertain sunshine became more frequent and my spirits began to lift. As I felt the child stir in my womb I looked forward to a new beginning. Cautiously I began to share Gaetano's belief that it was possible to put the past behind us. I would never forget but I would try to concentrate on the living rather than the dead. Even Signora Giovanelli could not live forever. This comforting thought brought a smile to my face. It was also possible that Gesualdo would stay in Ferrara permanently and I could remain in Venice. If this was to be my destiny it might not be so bad.

I was thinking these thoughts as I walked by the Rio della Sensa one bright morning remembering how different my feelings had been on my first day in Venice. I looked down at the water, green and sluggish as always, and saw the faint stirring of one of its citizens. One day I would learn not to shudder when one of the large water rats emerged, blinking in the sunlight, to perch on the walkway, staring at me in a way that reminded me of my mother-in-law.

I thought of the handsome, sleek, shining gondola that would soon be ours. The future would be assured, thanks to Donna Maria. I carried on walking, lifting my face to the sun and imagining myself for an instant back in the golden south. Around me the everyday noises of the city continued. A small, grey tabby cat brushed around my ankles and I tried to bend down to stroke it but I could not reach across my bulging stomach. Laughing, I moved on and the cat attached itself to another passer-by.

A loud bang came from the direction of the Grand Canal and a flaming brand shot up into the sky. The casino was in that direction; no doubt some festivity was going on. I felt strangely light-headed as I walked home to start preparing a meal. I could hear Gaetano's voice saying, as always, 'prepare some soup, dear heart.'

They came just as the soup was almost ready; our neighbour Federico and some of the other gondoliers. They shuffled their feet for some time unable to look me in the eye. In the background Signora Giovanelli began to make a harsh, keening noise.

Finally, they blurted out the story. A barge full of gunpowder coming from the Arsenale had collided with Gaetano's gondola. Somehow the gunpowder had ignited, possibly from the lantern that was kept burning on the prow at all hours. There was an explosion. Gaetano was dead.

29

The Lost

The moon hung low over the city turning the rooftops to silver and enfolding Venice's cats in a pale, spectral light. The sound of lapping water was never absent but in the little rio beneath my window I was conscious only of the occasional clunk of a moored boat. I knew what lay beyond the small inlet, the wide waters of the Grand Canal busy with swaying gondolas and their excited passengers living their night lives. Gondoliers would be lining up their boats outside the casinos, but one of them would be missing.

Gaetano's friends wore fluttering black ribbons on their sleeves as a mark of respect. The little room where the three of us had lived together was still full of the heavy scent of white lilies, although the flowers were withered and drooping.

I sat looking up at the moon. My husband had been buried three days ago. For a moment, the blazing white ball of the full moon looked spotted and striped with darkness. The stripes became recognizable figures standing in the silver orb, Donna Maria, Fillide, Sarah, Gaetano – all the people I had ever loved or cared about. Then the black stripes dissolved and became merely black clouds crossing the moon. Another barge banged against a mooring pole and an animal somewhere gave a mournful howl.

It was two in the morning but sleep had deserted me once again. I had slept little since Gaetano's death, despite a feeling of deep exhaustion. I was eight months pregnant and the discomfort of my body, blending with the despair in my heart, was unbearable. The child within me kicked vigorously as if it was impatient to join me, to be part of the sorrow and wonder of Venetian life.

My mother-in-law and I still lived together in the same room but already we led separate lives. We barely spoke or glanced at each other. Signora Giovanelli spent most of her time rocking in her chair and moaning with her shawl over her head. Federico and the other gondoliers had collected a little money for me – enough to last until the baby was born. I did nothing very much. I simple walked whenever I could or sat at the window gazing at nothing.

My walks took place mainly at night. I did not want to be stared at because of my bulk or pitied by watching neighbours. Gaetano had never allowed me to wander alone, saying that the streets were not safe for women despite the presence of the Civil Guard. Now there was nobody to know or care what happened to me.

I fell into an almost trance-like state in which I wandered through a magical city full of winged lions and carved dragons that mocked and threatened me silently. I walked everywhere, seldom taking to the water. I remembered how surprised I had been when I first arrived in the city to discover that it was possible to walk so much. I had expected to be constantly afloat. Now I knew I could linger in these narrow alleys and byways forever, never finding my way home again. Where was home now? Home was Gaetano and he was gone.

I had no fear of cut-throats; I was in a daze of grief. When I grew tired I would lean against a parapet for a moment looking into the dark recesses of a small, hidden canal. Sometimes the black prow of a gondola would glide past silently bearing its hooded, caped passengers on mysterious errands.

When I thought about Gaetano's sudden death I began to doubt that it was an accident as I had been told. Could it have been intended as a warning for Jacob da Costa who had not yet left the city? He was the owner of the gondola and this was strictly unlawful for Jews. The Council of Ten had allowed it for reasons of its own. Perhaps something had happened to change the situation. Could that something be connected to the kidnap of Sarah da Costa?

I turned these things round and round in my mind, but nothing made sense and my head began to ache. All I knew was that my husband's life would not have mattered to the authorities. He was just an ordinary working man.

Then I was consumed with guilt because I had not given Gaetano the pearls, had not insisted that he purchase his own craft as soon as possible. Once again someone dear to me had suffered because of my cursed character. As I wandered around thinking these thoughts a wail of grief would escape from my mouth, startling passers-by.

I stumbled over beggars who cursed me, then sometimes told me to take care when they saw my stomach. During the day, little children wearing coloured stockings and shawls played in corners as I passed by and the child within me would suddenly stir, kicking to remind me of its presence.

I felt the soul of this city for the first time as I wandered – the laughing, weeping, dreaming and singing, the shouts and groans of the desperate in the casinos, the chanting from the temples in the ghetto and the tolling of the Maragona. Whenever a gondola glided by under a little, humpbacked bridge I would watch the gondolier at the prow, his feet turned out and his shoulder slanted at a graceful angle as he polled the craft along. In every one of them I saw Gaetano's face and another wail of grief would shake my body.

One day, I wandered into the church of the Miracoli, reliving our times there and my husband's firm grasp on my arm as we made our wedding vows. The smell of jasmine was in the air and I could see Mistress Sarah waving her boy's cap in the distance.

The scene shimmered in the air before me and was gone, replaced by a vision of the sunlit Bay of Naples. Then I remembered that this strange, beguiling, sinister, watery city was not my home. Why had I come to Venice? I had achieved nothing. Gesualdo, the Prince of Venosa, still lived and prospered while my cursed presence had destroyed more innocent people. Anyone I cared for would perish. It must be written in my stars.

Another week or two must have passed in this way,

unreal and distant, as if I saw the world through a thick mist. I was brought back to reality by the onset of labour pains. Federico's wife found me collapsed outside the house and helped me indoors.

'The baby is coming early; it must be the shock of Gaetano's death' she told Signora Giovanelli who stood by in a daze. I was put to bed and the room quickly filled with Venetian matrons who bustled around preparing herbal concoctions and other necessities for the birth. One woman prepared the many religious charms and amulets that would be sewn into the swaddling clothes for protection. The labour was long and hard and I remember hearing my own screams echoing around the small room. When the baby was finally born I heard a thin, mewling cry before I floated into darkness.

In my dreams, I saw scenes I had often witnessed in the city as the native Venetians taught their children to swim. The parents tied long strings around the little bodies and launched them into the smaller canals while they controlled the strings from the shore. The whole family and passers-by would shout encouragement and instructions to the child. Grief overwhelmed me as I remembered that Gaetano would never teach our child. How would he or she survive in this water city? I could not swim but my child must learn somehow.

Then the dream changed again to one I knew well. I was in a gondola on the black lagoon. The skeleton of Donna Maria lay beside me and I held a dead child in my arms.

When I woke again it was still dark. I heard my mother-in-law shooing the other women out of the room. She bent over me saying that more than twenty-four hours had passed.

'The baby?' I whispered. The signora shook her head sadly. 'The child was a girl. She did not survive - she was too small.' I turned my head to the wall and let the darkness return.

Later, when I recovered a little and sat up I asked to see the body of my child.

'No, no!' I wailed at the old woman when she said that she had already taken the infant for burial.

'It was for the best. I sent for the priest and he agreed to take the infant away. I accompanied him, of course. Alas! There was no money for a headstone. The poor child was buried in a pauper's grave. I had only sufficient money for a mass. May Our Lord, the Blessed Virgin and all the saints have mercy on the babe.' She retreated from my side, spilling the soup she had prepared as I sat up and tried to seize a handful of her skirt.

'I must see her…take me to her, please.' I choked and howled and threw myself back on my pallet. Then, as there was no reaction from the old woman I felt my mood change from despair to fury. I cried out at her again. Why could she not understand my misery?

'I know you have hidden my baby. Where is she? I don't believe she is dead.' I sank back again, exhausted by my efforts. Signora Giovanelli refused to meet my eyes although I knew she was watching me constantly. As the days went by I recovered my strength and my suspicions of the old woman grew. I could not accept her story. She had given the neighbours the same tale. The baby had died soon after birth and had already been buried. She had taken the child alone after the neighbours withdrew. They trooped in to lament and weep with me but I remained dry-eyed and silent. Because I had never held the baby in my arms or looked at her face I could not accept her death. My little Maria Laura Domenica was still alive somewhere.

'It's natural to feel that way after the loss of a child.' Federico's wife tried to comfort me. 'I lost two myself, one at birth and one at eighteen months old. It is God's will.' I shook my head. 'I know she is still alive.'

I became convinced that my mother-in-law and the priest had taken the child, even given her to another woman. She was hand -in- glove with Father Constantino at San Geremia. I imagined her telling him that I was unfit to be a mother, that I had no husband to support me. I brooded on this for hours, fear and rage boiling inside me.

When I could bear it no longer I left the house secretly and went to the church, crying out to see the parish priest. After many minutes, a nervous-looking young curate appeared.

'Father Constantino is away on a mission. How may I assist you?' I threw myself at him, clutching his arm, shaking it and shouting, 'Where is my child? What has he done with her? I will not leave until you tell me the truth.'

The young man looked more nervous than ever. He was unused to dealing with distraught women. As I poured out my story he tried to prise my fingers away, but I had the strength of several women at that moment. He wrinkled his nose at my unwashed body and shabby appearance as I held onto his arm like a dog with a bone.

'Your child is not here,' he protested. 'We do not keep kidnapped infants on these premises. You have lost your wits, woman. If the child died at birth she was brought here to be buried.'

'Show me her grave,' I screamed, still scrabbling at his gown and pulling him towards the door.

'If she was buried in a pauper's grave there may not be a marker yet,' he protested. 'I cannot tell; you must wait until Father Constantino returns. I cannot help you.' He managed to free himself, pushed me away and disappeared rapidly into the church.

I ran into the small graveyard nearby as heavy rain began to fall. Frantically, I scrabbled in the mud among the graves marked only with small wooden crosses and those unmarked, signifying a pauper's resting place. When I found a fresh mound that looked smaller than the others, as if it might be a child's grave, I began to tear at the earth with my bare hands as the rain poured down.

Moments later, two gravediggers appeared, alerted by a horrified passer-by. They dragged me away and I screamed until my throat was raw. I must have collapsed again for when I woke I was lying on my pallet and my mother-in-law was attempting to remove my saturated clothing with the assistance of Federico's wife.

'She has lost her mind. My troubles are as wide as the sea.' I heard the familiar, sanctimonious voice as I closed my eyes for a second.

'Don't say that,' urged the neighbour. 'She is still recovering from the birth and the tragedy. It might have been better if you had let her see the infant.' Signora Giovanelli bridled at this criticism insisting that she had acted in the best interests of everyone.

'I know my duty, thanks be to God, even when I am overcome with grief.' The neighbour left the room defeated by the old woman's armour of self-righteousness. I sat up and glared at her.

'I know you have hidden her. Did you give her away or smother her in her cradle, you old witch?' She waved her hand dismissively.

'That is a wicked thing to say, but I forgive you, my daughter. You are raving. I will bring you a calming drink.'

'I will not eat or drink anything from your hand – Mother,' I sneered. With a sudden movement, I leapt from my bed and knocked the old woman to the floor attempting to strangle her. I was beside myself with fury and despair. She writhed and squirmed until I sat across her body, squeezing her throat until her face began to turn blue.

'Now, the truth,' I said, 'or you will not live to see another day, as God is my witness.' I relaxed my grip a little allowing her to speak. She choked for a moment, her colour changing from purple to red and then to white. She bared her teeth in a triumphant grin.

'I gave her to the nuns at San Eufemia. They will take care of my son's child. What can you do for her? You are nothing!'

A finger of ice prickled down my back. I clutched at my chest remembering that the pouch containing the pearls had been removed from my body during labour. The signora read the look on my face. 'I gave the nuns one of the pearls as alms for their work,for God's work.' Her eyes were focused on a box in the corner of the room. When I opened it I saw that it was empty. She was lying to me. I stood over the old woman's body as she lay on the floor.

'I know what you tried to do with my underskirt, you old bitch. But it wasn't mine, it belonged to Mistress Sarah. The curse passed to her. May it come back to you.' Rage overwhelmed me. I kicked her again and left the house. I had to find the truth somehow.

When I returned late that night after walking aimlessly in the darkness, the signora was asleep on her pallet. I tossed and turned into the small hours. As the church bells tolled two in the morning my mother-in-law rose, dressed hurriedly and went out muttering in an agitated manner. I turned over and fell asleep.

30

Extract from the Journal of
Don Carlo Gesualdo, Prince of Venosa

June 2. 1595

My wife, the Princess Leonora, has given birth to a healthy boy, Deo Gratias. The child will be called Alfonsino in honour of the Duke. At least my wives, unsatisfactory in other ways, have presented me with sons rather than daughters.

Leonora is entirely obsessed with the child and I can now consider returning permanently to the South in a few months. I grow weary of travelling away from home. My music room calls to me from the castle in Gesualdo.

The Duke and my brothers-in-law continue to be civil to me but I suspect that my wife is poisoning their minds against me. No doubt she plays the maltreated wife. I have heard rumours that I am considered excessive and loquacious in my manner. My valet, Bardotti, tells me everything. It seems that my nocturnal activities also meet with their disapproval. May they all rot in hell!

*****

31

Venetia

'Do you mean to tell me that you can shed no light on this tragedy, signora?' Father Constantino adjusted his black robes over a prominent paunch and stared accusingly at me.

'Your own mother-in-law, surely you knew her mind to some extent?' I leaned wearily against the wall while the priest occupied the only chair in the room. I stared back at him refusing to be cowed.

'I knew nothing of my mother-in-law's thoughts. She disliked me and we seldom spoke. As for tragedy, there has been plenty of that in this house in recent months.'

The priest from San Geremia fiddled with his rosary beads and had the grace to look slightly ashamed.

'I did not mean to sound harsh, my child. I know that you have suffered grievously; first the death of your husband, and now Signora Giovanelli is gone.' He made no mention of my baby. Did he know what had happened to her, I wondered?

I stared down at the priest's feet shod in sturdy black boots. Did he really think that I mourned the loss of that dreadful woman? Automatically I crossed myself as the priest muttered an Ave and rose from the chair.

'It is a terrible thing,' he continued, 'Signora Giovanelli was a valued member of our congregation, a most devout woman. It is unimaginable that she would commit such a terrible sin. Suicide! May the Lord preserve us!' He crossed himself again.

'She must be buried in unhallowed ground, I fear.' I repressed a shrug of indifference and remained silent.

'I suppose it is possible that she could have fallen into the canal accidentally?' the priest asked hopefully. This time I gave a genuine shrug.

'Perhaps she was pushed,' I said in an even tone. The priest looked horrified.

'What are you suggesting, signora? Such a good woman could not have had any enemies. It must have been an accident, a tragic accident. I might be able to convince the church authorities of that. Then we could, at least, give the poor woman a Christian burial.'

I nodded and muttered a word of thanks wishing that the wretched little man would leave. I doubted the Patriarch would believe such a story. Old women who were native Venetians did not usually fall into the Grand Canal in the middle of the night by accident. I could not accept that the old witch had taken her own life. She was far too selfish for such an action. Perhaps, after all, it was possible that she had been attacked and thrown into the water. I said nothing of this to the priest.

I did not tell him that I had been awake on that night

when the signora had dressed and left the house as the church bells chimed two o'clock. I made no attempt to stop her or to ask her where she was going. Gaetano's mother had fled from the room pursued by her personal demons. Her body had been fished from the canal the following day. She had condemned herself just as Gesualdo's actions had condemned him.

For me, after the agony of the loss of my child, the worst discovery had been that I no longer possessed Donna Maria's pearls. The pouch was around my neck once more but it was empty. My mother-in-law had removed the two remaining pearls while I slept after the birth. My sleep had been deep and full of bad dreams. I could not imagine why she wanted the third pearl. Why would anyone steal such a thing simply to die with it? I was convinced that the pearl was now at the bottom of the Grand Canal. The signora had been full of spite until the end.

After he had taken his leave, I sat quietly by the little window watching the life of the canal as I had done so many times since I arrived in Venice. My life had completed another circle of Purgatory - or so it seemed to me. Whenever I allowed myself to think about my lost child I felt a dull pain somewhere under my ribs. I had to persuade the nuns to give her back to me. The loss of the pearls, grave though it was, did not compare with her loss. I shook off my torpor and dressed carefully before hurrying through the streets in the direction of St. Mark's Square.

The great piazza had always been my favourite place in the city. Lost in the throng of people, the sociability, the hawkers crying their wares from various stalls, beggars showing their sores to passers-by, and the processions of important people passing into the cathedral I was transported out of my own life for a few moments.

It was always carnival time in the Square. It was always carnival time in Venice if you stayed away from the dark alleyways in the more sinister areas of the Serenissima.

I remembered the Grand Canal and I shuddered as the sound of the explosion that killed Gaetano echoed in my head. The waters of the city had also claimed my mother-in-law's life and somewhere in that secretive and unwholesome place my tiny child was sleeping alone, far from her mother.

Thinking of these things was enough to start the tears flowing again. What a sight I must have been, shrouding my face with a black shawl to hide my bitter tears while revellers shouted joyfully all around me. I recalled the time we had spent on the lagoon with the soft, lustrous light reflecting the towers and bridges of this magical city. Gaetano often told me that the lagoon was quite shallow but when I looked into the water I seemed to lose myself and all the palaces of Venice in its infinite depths.

I remembered the journey home from Burano after our wedding night. It was soon after dawn and a solitary fowler stood in a sandalo with his bow and arrow poised as the birds flew by leisurely in the pearlescent sky. Gaetano pointed at the heavens and cried, 'See, my love, the Venetian light is like no other. That is why so many great artists come here to paint.' I smiled, wondering how he could know this when he had never left the city.

I had told him of the beauty of Noto and the splendours of Naples, but he was not impressed. Venetians know they live in the most extraordinary place in the world – a city built on a forest in the sea. When I told him about the orange groves in Noto he retorted that, 'A Venetian sunset can make you weep.'

In one corner of the square a troupe of travelling players was performing. From my position, I could see the makeshift stage they had set up with the giant bronze horses of St Mark's in the background. There were about a dozen players in the group including some women, I noted.

I laughed as Arlecchino in his cat mask alternately cajoled and insulted the crowd to great applause. It was the first time I had laughed for many weeks and I lost myself completely in the story and the action for a brief half hour. The audience joined in fully, shouting encouragement, booing and hissing the villain and whistling at the female players. Two clowns gambolled around, turning somersaults and falling over each other, pursued by Arlecchino waving his slapstick.

Eventually, the play was over. The villain had been routed, the lovers re-united and Pantalone, the old merchant, humiliated. The actors took their bows to loud applause and the crowd dispersed. I lingered for a few minutes in the sun watching the actors packing up their props. One of the clowns smiled and waved to me as I wandered off.

I thought of all the wonderful sights I had seen in this city. My favourite was the Feast of the Redentore in July when a bridge of boats was built across the Guidecca canal to the Church of the Redeemer. Everyone in Venice, including the Doge, crossed the bridge to give thanks for the city's recovery from the plague. Gaetano had rowed me out to the lagoon where we had a fine view of the ceremony.

I began to weep again at the memory. I stifled a cry of anguish for the loss of the little family that had been mine for such a short time. Suddenly, I longed for my dead mother and the comfort I knew she would have given me.

I hailed people at random in the square, asking the way to the orphanage of San Eufemia. Most of them ignored me or laughed or pushed me away. Finally, a food vendor paused for a moment and gave me directions. My feet dragged as I approached the building. Its high walls and even higher towers frowned down at me confirming what everyone inside must know, that I was an unfit mother.

I put my hand momentarily into the lion's mouth set in the wall. This was where unwanted children were left anonymously, often by the city's prostitutes. But my mother-in-law had spoken with the sisters, had given them a pearl. Surely, they would see me... would allow me to tell my story?

I pulled at the bell, hearing the mournful clang somewhere inside the building. A nun eventually spoke through the lion's mouth.

'What is your business here?' I gave her my name.

'My mother-in-law brought my baby here recently without my permission. I must speak to the Mother Superior.' I waited for what seemed an interminable time until the door opened slowly and the nun beckoned me in.

After giving me a speculative look she told me to follow her down several long, silent corridors. She explained that the children were in another part of the building. As we crossed the cloisters I heard the faint sound of singing mingled with birdsong. It sounded so beautiful, so peaceful, yet this orphanage must harbour so much childish grief. I hurried after the nun. I hurried toward my baby.

32

San Eufemia

Mother Lucia, the convent superior, regarded me calmly as I stood shifting from foot to foot clutching my shawl to my chest. From her high, carved chair she took in my velvet gown, worn to create a good impression but much too fine for a peasant woman, matched with scuffed boots and an old shawl.

I wanted to explain that the gown was one of Sarah's given to me before she left the city. I wanted to tell her about Gaetano's death and my evil mother-in-law…about everything. It was some time before I could utter anything other than a series of stutters and a gasped, 'I want my child. Please give me back my child.'

The nun folded and unfolded her hands and clasped the large metal crucifix around her neck.

'You had better tell me the whole story.' She leaned back in her chair while I continued to shuffle my feet on the cold, tiled floor. There was no other seat in the room and I would certainly not have been offered one in any event.

When I had finished my story, she clasped her hands

again and regarded me with her piercing blue eyes. Her face had a smooth, waxy appearance unlike her old woman's hands which were knobbly and blue-veined like old cheese. I noticed these things automatically but the scene was unreal somehow, as if I was watching another woman begging for her baby.

'Tell me, my child, how will you support the infant if she is returned to you?'

'I have the means to earn my living,' I cried. I explained that the good sisters had trained me in herbalism. There was a flicker of interest in Mother Lucia's eyes at that. Then I told her that I had been working as a lady's maid, avoiding any mention that my employers were a murdered princess and a Jewish woman. The nun waved this aside. 'I do not see how you could care for a small child in such circumstances if you have no relatives to assist you.'

'My neighbours are very kind. They would help me.' The Mother Superior shrugged,' If you paid them, no doubt. You will be in dire poverty, I think. If you leave the infant with us she will have a future. She will be taught to read and write, she will be fed and clothed and raised by Holy Mother Church. In addition, she will be taught a useful accomplishment. If she proves to have musical talent her future could be bright. What can you offer her?'

Music…it followed me everywhere although I could not sing or play a note. Persistent melodies rang in my head, Gesualdo's ghastly madrigals, Gaetano's light-hearted gondolier songs, the chanting of the mass, even the tune the peddler had whistled in Sicily.

'There is the pearl…the pearl,' I cried. 'My mother-in-law gave it to you but it belongs to me. It will provide for me and my child.' The nun's face darkened. 'It was given as alms to the Church. It cannot be returned whatever the circumstances.'

So I had nothing, nothing at all.

'I cannot leave her,' I whispered. 'I have not even seen her face. She was taken from me at birth.' Mother Lucia looked intently at her hands and said,

'When a child is accepted within these walls there can be no more contact with the family until the child is grown. It is for the best. You may return for her then.' She rose and signalled to me to follow her. After a whispered conversation with another sister she led me to a high window overlooking the cloisters.

I looked down and saw a nun looking up at me. She held a small, white bundle. The nun pulled back a cover and held the bundle up to me, but I could not see the baby's face, we were too far away. I turned away with a sob and Mother Lucia touched my arm. 'It is for the best.'

When the stout doors of the convent had slammed behind me I collapsed under the lion's mouth opening, unable to move. Why had I not fought harder for little Maria? Because in my heart I knew I could not give her a life. My mother would have helped me. Why did she have to die and leave me cursed?

Suddenly, a voice whispered from the lion's mouth.

'Take this,' said the porteress. 'Mother Superior was given two pearls with your child. She should have told you as much.' A hand placed a small object in the mouth wrapped in paper. I took the packet and moved away, wandering around aimlessly, clutching the pearl.

Utterly defeated, I turned towards the Mole, where the masts of sailing ships towered above us to remind me of the world outside Venice. As always, I thought of Sarah and her fate. Where was she now, in faraway Constantinople among the Turks?

Suddenly, I was seized with an overwhelming longing to see Naples again, to return to the South. I had stayed long enough among cold northerners. If I could not make a home in Venice with little Maria then the city had nothing to offer me. I had to get away.

I looked towards the open sea. Somewhere over the horizon lay the Kingdom of Naples - and the Prince of Venosa. I would find the Dark Lord again. I would have my revenge. I would be revenged on all of them, the peddler, the prince, my mother-in-law, even the Mother Superior, the Church's representative, who had refused to give me my child. I beat my hands uselessly against the harbour wall. Then I took out the tiny package containing the pearl and looked at it. It connected me with Donna Maria. She had intended it to bring me good fortune and perhaps it would, despite everything. I watered it with a few more tears.

33

Commedia

I wandered back to the Piazza San Marco still in a daze of grief. I had little money and I did not know how I could travel back to Naples My last pearl had been returned to me, but I would never sell it.

The players had been giving another show and they were packing away their scenery and props. The man who had smiled at me before came over to where I stood, trying to wipe away tears.

'Hello,' he said, 'I noticed you before. You looked sad and we made you smile. I was glad of that. Now you look sad again.' I shook my head helplessly. 'I...I need to get back to Naples...'

'And you have no money?' He smiled again. 'Come and join us for a meal. We will eat before we prepare to journey south. My name is Nicolo Longhi,' he added.' I followed him, having nothing better to do. He introduced me to the players who greeted me in a friendly manner, asking no questions.

Soon we were tucked away in a tavern in the Arsenale

district, drinking wine and eating chicken. Again, for a short time I managed to throw off the heavy cloak of grief and join in the chatter.

People may think me shallow that I could do this so soon after losing my child for who knew how long, perhaps forever. They must understand that the only way I could live from that time was by concentrating on the moment. I had to place a chip of ice in my heart. My only ambition now was to reach Naples.

My meeting with the players was the most fortunate thing to happen to me in many months. When I told them I had skills in herbalism they invited me to join their party. They were leaving Venice and heading slowly south. They had need of someone to treat their afflictions, and to treat the old horse which drew the cart carrying their goods and props.

'The travelling life is a hard one,' said Nicolo. We have our share of sickness and fevers. You could be very useful to us. We can also teach you some tricks so that you can perform on stage.' My look of alarm made them laugh out loud.

'Anyone can learn tumbling and running around stage banging a drum,' said the man who played the doctor. 'Perhaps, in due course, we will reach Naples, God willing.'

We left Venice a few days later. As I stepped onto the barge that would transport us to the mainland, I drew my shawl over my head and hid my face so that my companions would not see the tears I shed. I was leaving my child in the water city. Would I ever see her again? 'I will come back, I will…I will,' I told myself as the city receded across the lagoon. 'I will come back for you when you are grown, I promise.'

My heart sank into my boots and my face must have appeared as grey as the rain clouds that suddenly bloomed overhead. Someone asked me if I was unwell. I turned my head away and muttered about being a poor sailor.

Looking back, that long journey south had an unreal quality, as if I was present in body, but not entirely in spirit. I had made this journey once before in reverse but more directly. This time, our passage was a slow, stopping expedition taking many detours through small towns and sleepy villages. Days and weeks passed marked only by dirty wayside inns, camp fires and the weather. Was it good or bad? Would the cart be stuck in a muddy ditch or would we suffer hunger and thirst in the endless countryside?

Sometimes we visited a real city. There we would play to unsophisticated audiences in the poorer districts. We received a mixed reception.

34

The Green Heart of Italy

I saw the beauty of Florence and the ancient ruins of Rome for the first and last time because we performed in those places. In Rome, I stood on the site of Fillide's burning, reliving my vision with pain and weeping. Nicolo was with me and he could not understand why I was so tormented. He caught me as I almost collapsed and tried to revive me with a little rough wine.

I had told him of my husband's death and now I explained about Fillide's burning. I did not burden him with the other tales of death and sorrow that were part of my life. He had shown me kindness and I could not repay him with such knowledge.

Most of the time we were not in the city. We travelled through lonely countryside stopping in small villages to perform in the market square, greeted with smiles and occasionally with stones and hostility and cursing from the village priest. We foraged for food catching rabbits for a delicious open-air stew, fishing in rivers and snaring birds. Nicolo was adept at bird snaring.

The troupe had travelled in Sicily in the past and they told me many things about my island that I did not know. But they had never visited Noto, beautiful Noto.

'Near Siracusa there is a cavern shaped like a giant's ear,' said Giacomo, the older man who played Pantalone. 'It is called the Ear of Dionysius after an ancient Greek ruler of Siracusa. The cavern contains a marvellous echo and we rehearsed there two or three times just to hear our own sounds.'

'Yes,' added Nicolo, the cavern was dug out and shaped by the Greeks. The polished walls made a wonderful backdrop for us. The local people said that the rulers of Siracusa tortured prisoners there so that their screams could be heard in the town, but that is just a story.'

'There are many stories on my island,' I muttered, 'and most of them are bad.'

We were rehearsing a play called The Jealous Old Man in which Pantalone had the chief role and the story revolved around his young wife and her lover and their efforts to outwit the old man. I had a small part as the daughter of the gardener. I could be entrusted with one or two lines but it was obvious that I had no talent as an actress. I preferred to sit near the old horse watching the players, and watching the audience, which was just as fascinating.

Our travels into the green heart of Italy were a revelation to me. I had spent little time in the country. I was always in a village or a city or a castle. Since my encounter with the peddler I had taken care to avoid the countryside, but now things were different.

Sometimes our play was not received well. The players would be downcast afterwards, especially if a rotten egg or two had been thrown or someone had complained that the female members were not pretty enough.

'No doubt the village priest will preach against us, just to complete the visit,' said Nicolo after one such performance in a small, mean village.

'What do they expect from us?' Pantalone cried. 'Do they think we are the Gelosi? If we were, we would not be appearing in this God-forsaken hell hole!' He explained that the Gelosi were the most famous commedia troupe in Italy. Its leading actors were famous and performed in all the greatest courts.

We sat around a meagre fire full of despondency, wishing ourselves among those elite players. The village was a poor one; there was no inn however flea-bitten, and the hard pressed, unfriendly villagers had not offered hospitality. The players reminisced about previous tours. Pantalone remarked that, 'Sometimes a local lord would invite us to perform for his court and treat us to a fine meal afterwards.' We gazed wistfully into the fire which could not decide whether to persevere or subside into smoke and ashes. Our supper had consisted of a thin vegetable soup and some stale bread.

'What is your favourite meal?' someone asked, and we spent a few minutes tormenting ourselves with descriptions of good food.

'Lamb stew and polenta with a glass of red wine,' I said when my turn came – 'and an orange from Noto,' I added for good measure. This led to calls for stories and descriptions of my favourite place. I dwelt on the good things with no mention of the peddler or the fate of Donna Maria.

'Why did you leave?' Nicolo asked. I told him that I had been dismissed from my lady's service in Naples when she remarried and they all sighed sympathetically. 'How did you come to Venice?' Nicolo persisted. I laughed lightly and said that I was a wanderer by nature just as they were. And with that they were content.

Nicolo had travelled abroad as far as Paris and even London.

'There are several theatres in London and a playwright called Shakespeare who has written some fine dramas. Women cannot perform there so boys take the female parts. Is that not strange?'

'Did you enjoy your stay there?' I asked. He shrugged and whistled into the darkness.

'The weather is foul and the food not much better. The people are uncouth and hostile to foreigners. They would curse me in the street for a papist and children would throw stones. Once I saw their Queen Elizabeth pass by on the river in great splendour, but the plays were the best I have ever seen.' We spent a miserable night before packing and leaving soon after dawn.

It was good to be in the company of friends as our little group made its way through the land at the old horse's gentle pace. Especially, I loved to watch the stars at night. Nicolo knew a great deal about them and we would watch them together. He explained that the constellations and the stars were named after the gods and heroes of the ancient Greeks. He showed me the Milky Way and pointed out Sirius the brightest star in the night sky. Once we saw Algol the demon star winking in the heavens. Nicolo said he had once seen a red moon over Pisa. Sometimes I saw a shooting star and thought again of those I had lost. Were they watching me from those shining places?

Our togetherness caused comment in the group and the friendly atmosphere began to change. I saw Nicolo only as a friend but I think his motives were different. I soon realised that he had a reputation in our little band when I was waylaid in the forest one morning by Faustina.

We had gone to make our toilette in private when the girl suddenly rounded on me accusing me of stealing Nicolo from her. Faustina played the young heroine in our dramas. She was not beautiful; her face was pitted with smallpox scars which she disguised with heavy makeup, but her eyes were extraordinary. As she stood close to me hissing venom, I looked into her eyes which were large and a vivid violet blue, fringed with dark lashes. Those eyes were as cold as ice.

'What do you want with Nicolo? He was mine until you came. You are too old for him.' I tried to explain that I had no romantic interest in him but that was the worst thing I could have done. Faustina repeated my words to Nicolo triumphantly, and he rounded on me in fury.

'I thought you were my friend,' I told him. 'I did not realise you needed a new woman so frequently.' He romanced every woman in the troupe and others who had left the group.

From that time on life became difficult for me. Pantalone took me under his wing as we made our way slowly and painfully through Italy. Most of the troupe confided their problems to me at various times. Perhaps they saw me as a healer. Nicolo ignored me as far as possible, but when we finally reached Naples he bade me a civil goodbye as I left the troupe and entered the city alone. After such a journey I felt as if I had reached the New World.

35

Extract from the Journal of Carlo Gesualdo, Prince of Venosa.

June 23.1606

Bardotti came to me this morning in my music room. His orders are not to disturb me unless it is a matter of the gravest importance. When I questioned him, he claimed to know that Don Emanuele was mismanaging the estates. He handed me a document of proof, as he called it, looking well pleased with himself.

I indicated my surprise because my son has barely begun his duties in this respect. He is still under my guidance. My valet, I suspect, is bored with his menial tasks and seeks to stir the waters. In the past, I have given him important tasks more fitting to a steward or scribe. He is almost too well-schooled for his station in life.

Since his involvement in the matter of my first wife and her lover he has become over familiar. My father warned me of the dangers of raising servants above their station. These people must be kept at a distance. Now he assumes that his great favour to me allows him a license I would not grant even to a member of my family.

So, this is how I am rewarded. Have I not kept him in my household all these years, well-fed, clothed and renumerated that he should now come to place a dagger in my heart?

I took the document from him, saying little. Bardotti went away full of self-importance. I sat looking out of the tower window for some time before writing a letter to Don Antonio commanding him to wait upon me urgently. He understands the importance of the family even though he is a bastard. His half-brother is my heir.

June 25

Don Antonio came late last night. We talked at length in the music room after the servants had gone to their beds. He will follow my orders implicitly, although he is not happy with the plans. The youth is still soft and untried in combat but my natural son knows better than to disobey me. He depends on me for everything.

June 27

Bardotti has departed for Naples on an errand for me. I told him he could visit his family for a day or two. He was most grateful. Don Antonio left last night with two horsemen.

June 30.

News has come that Pietro Bardotti, formerly known as Malitiale, has fallen victim to footpads on the road. I have told everyone that he died suddenly of cholera, therefore his body will not be returned to the castle. I am told he made an excellent cadaver. Ah well, he was growing too old for the work. Now I must search for another valet. Don Antonio had returned safely and I have rewarded him for carrying out this commission.

Now I must turn my mind to the problem of my heir. I must seek a suitable wife for him. There is little point in looking to the d'Este family now that the Duke is dead. As for the Neapolitan nobility, the matter of my first wife still casts a long shadow. A foreign wife might be the solution here and one that would find favour with the Viceroy.

*****

36

The Spanish Quarter

When I reached Naples, I sought work at the Hospital for the Incurables where I was able to use my skills in herbalism. I was often called upon to visit the sick in the Spanish Quarter off the Via Toledo. Few women, or men would venture "up the mulberries" as they were still called. Once there had been rows of mulberry trees for the silk worm industry on the hillsides but now they were a warren of narrow, dank, dark, squalid streets sloping steeply upwards. The Quarter had been built to accommodate the Spanish troops of the occupying power.

When you went "up the mulberries" it was for a special matter, the bushes had been popular with lovers. When I went up it was for a different reason. Now these same streets swarmed with broods of sickly, emaciated children, barefoot, screaming little beggars. I was not afraid of these hordes. Perhaps I no longer cared greatly about what happened to me. The people were usually pleased to see me because I offered them what help I could for their wracking coughs, their fevers and fluxes and all manner of boils and pustules.

Sister Antony would have been pleased to see me making good use of her teaching.

The poor had little to hope for. Neapolitans placed their trust in San Gennaro, the city's patron. If his blood liquified twice yearly in view of the people things would not go too badly. If that failed there was always the use of magic, especially for sex – and in the background the Tramontana wind would blow as the accompaniment to their woes, causing men to stick knives into their wives and women to smother infants and poison their husbands' soup.

Via Toledo ran down a steep ravine all the way to the sea, shining silver in the distance. It was always filled with people, gaiety, trading, fighting, begging and danger, day and night.

For myself, I had sought refuge again in the area near where I had lived with Fillide. I took a room in a street on the high ridge overlooking the Santa Lucia district. That time with her seemed so long ago, several lifetimes ago.

When it rained the ravine below and Via Toledo itself became a raging torrent as water poured down from the hillside alleyways. As I lay on my thin straw mattress with its one worn cover I could hear the drumming of the rain - a deluge that brought clouds of water vapour into my dingy room on that narrow street and made everything smell of damp and decay.

Sometimes, when life became too unbearable, I would steal some poppy tincture from the hospital that had been steeped in alcohol for six weeks. I took only the smallest amount and I felt shame at my actions, but I did it anyway.

The tincture was reserved to ease the pain of the dying and the agonies of the injured. My agony was of a different kind, compounded of hunger and utter weariness and the knowledge that I had returned to the South fruitlessly.

All I knew of the prince was what Carnero told me. We still met occasionally when he came to the city. Unless I could overcome my fears and return to the castle I would never fulfil my vow. When my fear and cowardice became too much for me to bear, when the wind and rain buffeted the walls and my bones ached from hours of back-breaking work, I swallowed the tincture with a glass of wine and took to my bed.

I closed my eyes and I was borne out to sea, over the shining Bay of Naples, far out on a magic oriental carpet like the ones in the palace in Palermo. I was flying to the New World, a place full of rainbow-hued birds and strange, flowering trees; a place where time had no meaning. There was no night and no fatigue. The endless golden sun shone down on me as I entered a building shaped like a vivid pink flower.

I realized that it was a pink flower of gigantic size and I was wandering along its filament tunnels while invisible instruments played music that ravished the senses. Here was no beginning and no end. I was playing in paradise and a child was holding my hand. I knew it was my daughter. We walked out of the flower and down to the bluest sea.

I woke the next morning after the longest sleep I had enjoyed for many months. Hunger gnawed at my innards and it was still raining. My mouth was as dry as a Sicilian hillside in summer but my mind was peaceful and calm for a while.

The Spaniards' grip on the city was as strong as ever. Their ceremonies and rituals were imprinted on our psyche. I remember the customs they celebrated during Holy Week. On Good Friday I watched as noblewomen in black carriages followed the penitents and the Mysteries in procession. Their carriages were black and their costumes were black. I caught a glimpse of these women with their gold trimmed, blood-red veils. The men folk followed on horseback throwing white sugar candy skulls into the carriages for the women to enjoy while the penitents flogged themselves with steel tipped ropes. Even in Sicily I could not remember seeing such things.

I was not surprised to hear from Carnero that Don Giulio Gesualdo had died. He was as bad as any member of that family, lustful and mean-spirited. Neither was I surprised that he contracted the French pox. If he had followed my prescription he would have obtained some relief for his eyes. Take the stalks, petals and roots of the Iris flower, distil over low heat and use the liquid to bathe the eyes frequently.

I would never forgive him for betraying my mistress, but I know that if he had not told the prince, then someone else would have done.

Life in Naples was terrible at that time. The city teemed with people and refugees, there was no food and prices were sky high. I had to show a ration book to get a little bread. My bones were poking through my shrunken skin. This was my condition when the next stage of my life began.

37

Extract from the Journal of
Don Carlo Gesualdo, Prince of Venosa

June 17 1606

Sad news has reached me concerning my esteemed uncle Don Giulio Gesualdo.who has been much afflicted of late. His eyes became inflamed to the point that he was unable to read or even to see his path. He continued in this state for some weeks and then developed small red blisters over his entire body.

His doctors gave him various treatments which were of little use. They told him he had contracted the French disease but he vehemently denied this, ascribing his afflictions to witchcraft.

A distinguished physician from Rome advised him to take lignum vitae and after using this treatment for some time he recovered much of his strength.

While he was still somewhat weak he acquired a magnificent black horse and spent hours riding it through marshland whereupon he fell ill again with fever. While in this weakened state he endeavoured to ride again and was thrown from the horse. He broke his leg in three places and died soon after.

I was not able to visit him before his death due to my own frailty. May he rest in peace, Miserere Domine. I have had masses said for his soul at Santa Maria delle Grazie.

It was through my uncle's good offices that I learned the truth about my first wife.

Part Three

38

The Artist

I moved slowly away from the shadowed entrance to the church of San Domenico Maggiore, drawing my shawl across my face as I moved into the piazza. Even though Gesualdo and his followers were not in the city I could not shake off my fear that he wanted me dead, that someone would recognize me.

This feeling made me angry and I silently scolded myself. Why would anyone remember me? It was the year 1606. I was forty years old, as far as I knew; grey haired and with a lined, weather-beaten face. There was little sign of the dark haired, wide-eyed Sicilian girl who had run away from the Palace of San Severo so many years before.

I sat down on the stones near the beggars' corner of the piazza staring at that same palace which had changed little over the years. I fiddled with the fringe of my shawl staring in disgust at my red, calloused hands, testimony to a few more years of drudgery. Nobody noticed me. Soon I would leave for a less fashionable corner of the city where I felt safer. I muttered a farewell to my mistress under my breath as I glanced back at the church. It was the sixteenth anniversary of the murder and I had paid my respects at Donna Maria's tomb once again.

The palace was silent and shuttered. The local people naturally believed that it was haunted. The ghost of the murdered woman was said to flit around the courtyard in a white gown wailing and crying. I did not believe this for a moment. I was sure that Donna Maria rested quietly in her grave. Hadn't I prayed enough for her over the years?

As I stood up to leave a man entered the piazza followed by two boys carrying several awkwardly shaped parcels between them. The man was stocky, very dark and had an excitable manner. With his narrow forehead and thick, curling hair he could have been a Sicilian. To my dismay he walked over to me and sat down. The boys dumped the parcels beside him and wandered off.

The man carried a melon which he split open with his dagger spilling out the vivid fruit. He offered a slice to me remarking that it looked like a gaping wound. Disgusted, I started to move away but he caught my arm and urged me to sit down. I sat back, willing him to go away. Suddenly, the man seized my cheeks with his sticky, juice covered hands and turned my face towards him, ignoring my furious struggles.

After inspecting my face, he released me saying, 'You would make a good model. Your face has a certain quality of stillness - strong, yet with sad eyes. You would do for the woman in my *Crucifixion of St Andrew*. I have a commission from the Viceroy. You'll get fed and have a place to sleep.'

He tossed me a few coins. 'Here's something on account. You can travel to the Colonna Palace tomorrow. That's where I have my studio.' He gave me a wolfish grin and returned to the melon.

I spat venom at him, poised to fling the coins back in his face. So, he thought I was a whore despite my grey hairs? Only prostitutes modelled for artists. Then I remembered that since I had left my work at the hospital I had very little money. I looked at the man more closely.

'What's your name...are you a famous artist?' He laughed and threw the melon rind over his shoulder.

'I am the greatest artist in all Italy. My name is Michelangelo Merisi and I am from Caravaggio.' He regarded me seriously for a moment. 'You are safe with me. I generally prefer boys!' He laughed, a peculiar high-pitched scream, and began to pick his teeth with the dagger. The boys returned to pick up the parcels and the artist prepared to leave as I stood there, undecided.

He moved away then spoke over his shoulder, 'I'll make you immortal in my paintings! Now I must speak to the Prior here. The good friars of San Domenico want me to paint a Flagellation of Christ for the church.' He handed me the remaining slice of melon and turned away. I called him back and seized his arm.

'I need the work you are offering me,' I said urgently, 'but it is not safe for me to spend time near San Domenico. I only come here once a year to pray at my mistress's tomb.' Merisi looked puzzled; 'The painting will be done at my studio in the Colonna Palace, there is no need for you to come to the church.' He looked at me with half-closed eyes. 'What have you done that is so terrible?' I swallowed hard and lowered my voice, staring down at the red juice trickling over my hands.

'My master murdered my mistress here in San Severo. I'm sure he wants me dead because I saw it all. ' I pointed across at the palace gates. 'It happened there, sixteen years ago today.'

The artist screamed with laughter, drawing all eyes to him. I cringed and buried my face in my hands. This was a man who couldn't help drawing attention to himself; the worst possible company for me. He slapped me painfully on the back.

'You are a foolish woman! No-one would be interested in you after so many years.' I shook my head. 'Princes have long memories and murder is always murder.' He gestured at the massive bulk of the church.

'San Domenico Maggiore is a strange place, you know. It's something of a haven for those who fall foul of authority and for those who are rebellious by nature. Perhaps that is why your lady was taken there for burial. Did you know that the heretic monk Giordano Bruno was here a few years ago?' I shook my head. A note of bitterness crept into his voice. 'I knew him and I saw him burned in Rome, the poor bastard.' I whispered, 'Someone dear to me was burned in Rome.'

The man I would come to know as Michele told me that he would arrange everything for me. I would be quite safe, he promised, adding casually, 'I've killed a man. These things happen.'

I slipped away having decided that although the artist was a wild fellow I had no feeling of unease in his company after those first few moments. It was possible that fate intended our paths to cross. Why else would a poor woman like me have been taken up by the most famous artist in all Italy?

Before I took up Michele's offer I did something I had not thought to do for many years. I sought out a local woman who read the cards. I had watched Fillide reading them for her clients so many times – and for herself when she saw her death written there. Sometimes she would offer to read mine, but I had always refused with a shudder after that first reading when she had predicted the murder. Was I not cursed already, cursed from birth? I did not need to hear more bad news about my future life.

Now…now things were different. I sensed a great change coming, a final drama to be lived through. Somehow, I knew that Michele would play a part in this drama but there was only one question I wanted to ask.

'Will I find my daughter again?'

The woman spread the cards out in a fan shape, choosing a Court Card of the Minor Arcana to represent me. She shuffled the cards and laid them out in groups of three. She examined my past life and character, my emotional life and my desires. I told her what she needed to know without going in to too much detail. It was not possible to trust many people in Naples. When I asked her the important question she paused a long time before repeating Fillide's words, 'Your hand is a very bad one.'

'But the future, my daughter, what do you see?' The

woman folded the cards in one sweep of her hand. 'There is some light in the future for you, some happiness. That is all I can tell you.' I was bundled out of the room while she looked anxiously along the deserted street. I was angry with myself for giving her my last coins. I had learned little enough, but I clung to those words "some light, some happiness."

I arrived in Chiaia at the Palazzo Colonna with my small bundle of possessions, just a stone's throw from the Piazza Carita on the edge of the Quarters. There I found an assortment of street people already installed. This unlikely group was presided over by Cecco, the artist's former model and, some said, his lover. He was an imperious youth who had made a good living selling his body to gentlemen on the streets of Rome, trading on his cherubic appearance and almost feminine allure.

And so, I was back in the area where Donna Maria's doomed love story began, although not in the same building. I found that the life of an artist's model suited me very well. When I modelled as the woman in the *Crucifixion of St Andrew* I was dismayed to find that Michele had given me a large goitre on my neck and even more wrinkles than I already had.

'But your beautiful, sad eyes are there too,' he assured me. Once, I modelled for St. Anne wearing a fine, dark blue silk shawl that covered my head and upper body. A gleam of white undershirt showed here and there but the light and shadow thrown by the silk was perfectly captured by Michele, reminding me of nights in my native Sicily.

In the studio he explained to us how he achieved this effect of chiaroscuro.

'Do you know about the camera obscura?' We were all sitting around in the studio and we shook our heads in unison.

'Look!' Michele commanded. He set up a mirror at one end of the room before standing in the strong sunlight pouring through the window. We watched from the shadows and Michele's image appeared upside down in the lens against the dark background with the facial colours standing out in sharp contrast. Someone whispered,

'witchcraft!' under his breath but Michele laughed and sent out for more wine. He was able to paint these strong shadows and colours directly onto the canvas. I never saw him draw or sketch anything. The effects were greatly admired by other artists in Naples who all tried to copy them.

When I heard that the painting of the *Childhood of the Virgin* in which I modelled for St.Anne was commissioned by Archbishop Gesualdo I felt the usual trickle of fear in my spine. The second mention of the Gesualdo name came as an even bigger shock.

Outside in the streets famine had the city in its grip once again. Priests and monks wandered around calling for the people to repent their sins while the starving called for bread. It was said that not a dog or a cat remained alive in the city. Fortunately, rats were always plentiful in Naples. Once, I saw Cecco pick up a scrap of bread from the gutter, bless it and eat it while looking guiltily over his shoulder. I did not blame him, the young were always hungry.

One morning Michele said, 'I have to make an expedition to the country to visit your musical prince. It seems he appreciates art as well as music.' He grinned at my stricken look before suggesting in his usual sarcastic way that I might like to accompany him. Moments later I found that I had agreed. I accepted that it was very unlikely that anyone would remember me, except Carnero, my dwarf friend, who would never betray me. Laura Scala no longer existed. I was Laura Maria Giovanelli, assistant to the artist. Together with Cecco and a boy who looked after the horses we set off for the castle.

39

Extract from the
Journal of Don Carlo Gesualdo

July 1607

I have decided to commission a painting from the renowned artist Caravaggio. He has been in Naples for some months under the patronage of the Colonnas. The painting will have a musical theme, naturally. The artist has been highly recommended by my esteemed brother-in-law Don Cesare d'Este who commissioned a Madonna of the Rosary for Modena two years ago.

Typically, Don Cesare paid only sixty scudi for this large work. Of course, the artist is a great villain who has been banned from Rome by the Pope, but sublime art must be recognized and nurtured. As an artist myself I understand this. My cousin, Ettore, has described to me the huge painting of the Seven Works of Mercy *painted by Caravaggio for the Pio Monte della Madonna di Misericordia. The crowded canvas celebrates our Neapolitan culture and is altogether a masterpiece, according to Ettore who is a connoisseur in matters artistic.*

I look forward to having something by this masterly rogue here in the castle. It will, of course, hang in the music room. I will pay the artist whatever he asks.

40

Return to the Castle

We spoke little on the journey; even Cecco ceased prattling and complaining. The country people stood in their barren fields like dumb animals, gravediggers worked day and night and church bells tolled at all hours. The soil looked brittle and lifeless as if it was taking revenge on the people who exploited it.

When I told my friends that the land around the village of Gesualdo was known for its putrid water they returned to the wine bottle with vigour. Nevertheless, Michele claimed he was glad to be leaving Naples behind.

'I hate the place,' he said. 'I hate the hordes of beggars, the strange nobility, and the Spanish soldiers lording it everywhere.' I think he really meant that Naples was not his beloved Rome. He was in exile.

The prince's lands came into view and we saw the sprouting stumps of trees he had cut down, fearing a surprise attack from the Carafa family after the murders. The fields were full of his beloved Calito horses – no signs of famine here, I noted.

As the cart rattled into the castle courtyard I was gripped with dread. I wrapped my shawl tightly around my head as Michele whispered, 'Show no fear.' He fingered his dagger on which the words' *no hope, no fear'* were engraved. I would try to live by the same maxim if I could.

As I entered the busy castle kitchen I was relieved to see that I recognized nobody from the old days. Within half an hour of our arrival I was told that the prince's valet, Pietro Bardotti, had died the previous year. No other servant would have remembered me. Carnero appeared later and greeted me politely, winking slyly when no-one was looking.

Michele went off to be received by the prince while I sat quietly in a corner listening to the kitchen gossip. I learned a great deal about the bad relationship between Gesualdo and his second wife, Donna Leonora, as well as the scandals among the large group of young men who served him. I heard about his musicians and his music but nothing about the events of sixteen years ago. The past was never mentioned in that household. The notoriously loose-mouthed servants did not repeat any gossip or anecdotes about that time, probably on pain of instant dismissal or worse.

It was as if Donna Maria had never lived, but there was one reminder of the past in the castle who could not be ignored or dismissed. That evening I crept into a shadowed corner of the minstrel's gallery as I had often done in the past. I saw the prince sitting at the head of the table, older, thinner, tetchier, but otherwise unchanged. Clad in black as always, his stick-like figure resembled an animated crotchet. Around him sat his musicians and cronies with the numerous young male attendants standing in the background. And there, seated to the left of his father, was Don Emanuele, the son of Donna Maria, heir to the Gesualdo title and the living image of his murdered mother.

I stared hard at the young man I remembered as an enchanting three year old toddling towards my outstretched arms in his mother's chamber. He had her golden hair and sensual lips. His figure was slim but strong, hardened by hunting and martial arts. He sat playing with his silver fork and carefully ignoring his father. The prince did not speak to his son at any time during the meal. I watched, transfixed, until a hand on my arm almost caused me to scream aloud.

One of the kitchen assistants had crept up to me. He saw me staring at Don Emanuele and whispered, 'That's Don Gesualdo's son. They hate each other, you know.' He sniggered as I whispered softly, 'Why? Why do they hate each other?'

'Don't you know?' The man stared at me.

'I'm a stranger here.' The man looked uneasy.

'No-one ever talks about it.' He lowered his voice still further so that I strained to hear it. 'The prince killed his first wife. He caught her with her lover – some duke or other. They were both stabbed and skewered like stuck pigs. She deserved it; no better than she should have been, that one!' He sniggered again and I clenched my fists in the darkness.

'Of course, it was way before my time here, but the valet Bardotti told me about it. He had a big hand in it, if you ask me. He had a big hand in everything that went on here.'

'But Bardotti is dead, isn't he? That's what the cook told me.'

'Yes,' he whispered, 'died last year of cholera, they say. He went down to Naples and never came back. There's some say he knew too much and the prince – well, he might have been worried about that.' The man's voice trailed away and he peered furtively over his shoulder. He had realized that he was talking to an outsider. He crept away, saying,

'It doesn't do to gossip about these things. It isn't healthy, if you know what I mean.'

Of course, I knew what he meant. I was a servant in that man's household, a servant of darkness. I did not feel pity for Bardotti. He was evil; he aided his master in all his deeds. He aided him too well and he paid the price. Gesualdo was not the trusting or forgiving kind.

I carried on watching the scene below. The servants cleared away the meal and the musicians filed into their places. They raised their instruments expectantly as the prince rose and tapped his silver fork against a goblet. Silence fell and then the first notes of a madrigal filled the air, *Bella Angioletta*.

Naturally, it was one of his own compositions. I had not heard it for many years but I knew it instantly. I looked at the woman sitting on the prince's right. Thin, dark-haired and long-nosed, she was as different from Donna Maria as the night sky was from the golden Sicilian sunshine. This was Leonora d'Este, still dressed in deep mourning for the death of her son. Her black gown glimmered with jet embroidery and white pearls shone at her neck contrasting with her sallow complexion.

Although she was from the north she looked as dark as any Neapolitan. Her husband ignored her and the rest of his family. His attention was focused entirely on the music and any conversation was directed at the master of the musicians or to his cousin, Ettore Gesualdo, who was sitting opposite him. I recognized Ettore immediately, the cousin with the waxed moustache and the beautiful singing voice. He looked older. They had all grown older. The young boy standing behind the prince's chair I identified from kitchen gossip as Castelvietro, known as Gesualdo's backwarmer.

Easing my cramped limbs for a second, I heard a sudden high-pitched scream. Crystal glasses pinged as silver forks knocked against them. Servants huddled around the prince while his family remained unmoved. The music master gesticulated angrily at the musicians.

'Enough! Enough!' he shouted. I realized that they had played a wrong note or two but it was enough to send their master into some kind of paroxysm, an attack of the breathlessness that afflicted him. He doubled up across the table and his servants prised him up and carried his gasping figure out of the hall. The musicians disappeared rapidly. Donna Polissena, the German daughter-in-law, continued to examine her nails, Don Emanuele poured more wine and Donna Leonora stared straight ahead lost in thought. I tip-toed away to my bed recalling that I had once heard the prince play a madrigal dedicated to a mole on Donna Maria's face. She had greatly enjoyed the piece.

41

A New Role

'I shall stay here,' I said to Michele as we stood by the cart in the castle courtyard a few days later. He shrugged, watching Cecco unload more equipment.

'You've changed your tune,' he remarked, 'but it's no business of mine. If you don't want to go back to Naples with me, that's fine. I have decided that I shall leave the city soon, anyway.' I nodded,' There is a position here for a lady's maid. I shall wait upon Donna Polissena.'

He laughed. 'That hussy. I should watch your step with her. There is a lot of gossip about the German woman – and none of it pleasant.' I shrugged.

'I don't care about her. You know I have other business here.' He nodded again, saying that he would stay for the few weeks needed to paint the portrait of Gesualdo and his musical companions. 'I think it will be one of my best minor works. I like the atmosphere in this place.' He grinned at my grimace of distaste.

'You must be the only person here who enjoys it,' I said. 'The atmosphere reeks of guilt and melancholy. The servants notice it; they don't stay long.'

'Just my kind of place.' Michele gave a wicked grin. 'And you are forgetting the music, my dear, the wonderful music of the Prince of Venosa. Isn't it worth staying here just to enjoy that?' He laughed heartily as I scowled and brushed past him.

Donna Polissena was a harsh taskmistress. I was accustomed to the ways of the aristocracy after so many years but I sometimes found my position intolerable. The other servants warned me, enjoying a good laugh at my expense when they heard that I had asked for the work. The news was the best joke they had heard for a month.

'By Satan's cock!' exclaimed the man I had met in the gallery that first night, 'There is no pleasing the German woman. She has a mouth as wide as hell's gateway and almost as dirty.' The cook smirked while pretending to be shocked. He patted my arm and wished me luck.

The steward, fondling his mangy cat as usual, gave me a knowing smile. 'Don't upset her,' he advised. Then he whispered in my ear, 'Remember Bardotti.'

Now Donna Polissena was standing in the middle of her bedchamber pale with rage, her face as blanched as the white blonde ringlets escaping from her cap. She tore at her bodice with tiny, plump hands that bulged over many rings as she screamed abuse at me in heavily accented Italian.

I had left the lid of the dowry chest open after placing the clean linen inside. I returned to close it but not quickly enough to prevent my employer from almost falling into a fit. A thin trickle of spit at the corner of the lady's mouth fascinated me as I watched from under lowered eyes. I was not afraid; I knew that few servants stayed with this woman longer than three months. It was only when Donna Polissena, screaming like a thing possessed, raised an arm to strike me that I retreated towards the open door.

As I stood in the doorway, poised for flight, a voice cut through the screaming and I felt another body standing so close to my own that warm breath filled my ear as he spoke.

'Perhaps I shall call a physician to attend you, daughter, before you do yourself a mischief.' With a quick movement, I was thrust aside and the prince strode into the chamber. He grasped his daughter-in-law's arm in a grip that made her squeak with pain. He fixed his black eyes on her and she quailed visibly.

'Upon my soul,' he drawled, 'I do believe I have married my son to a woman of unsound mind. I will arrange to have you bled, madam, to relieve these fits.' My presence was forgotten as the pair faced each other in mutual loathing. The prince dragged Polissena to the window and forced her head back, clutching the blonde curls.

'Your screams have reached me in my music room, vixen. You disturb God's work. You know I am composing music for the liturgy.' Polissena squeaked again but he raised his hand to stop her. 'Let us hope that the child you are carrying is a boy. Then at least you will have served some purpose in this household.' I watched them as history appeared to be repeating itself before my eyes. This time, he released his victim and rushed out pushing me aside again.

He had been dressed in black velvet, as always, with one

gold earring. I noticed that tiny seed pearls were scattered among his clothing in imitation of an Englishman, Sir Walter Raleigh. I had heard this name mentioned in the castle. I had no idea who Sir Walter was. All I knew of the English was that they were Protestants and, therefore, damned. Neither did I know why the prince admired this man.

'They both had wife trouble,' Michele commented.

42

Extract from the
Journal of the Prince of Venosa

Jan. 1608

My new daughter-in-law adds little to the well-being of this family and nothing at all to the peace of the house. Donna Polissena and my son are ill-suited but they must accommodate to each other. That is the true nature of the married state.

As for domestic matters, Emanuele deals with them reluctantly. Servants come and go; mostly they go — at least the ones who attend on Polissena go frequently. She has a new woman now, one who seems strangely familiar to me but I cannot place her.

My health continues to decline.

*****

43

A Resolution

I hid myself in the laundry room where Cecco found me when he came in search of fresh hose.

'They are all crazy in this place,' he remarked cheerfully, after I told him about the incident; 'especially the murderous prince with his strange music. It sounds like the screeching of a night owl with piles.' We both collapsed, laughing, and I felt a pang of regret that I would not be leaving with him and Michele. Soon I would have nobody to confide in or to console me with bad jokes and bad wine, only Carnero, who was growing morose with age.

'How long will the picture take to paint?' I asked.

'It could be a few weeks or a few days. It depends on how often the sitters pose.' Cecco looked gloomy, 'Just imagine weeks more in this boring hole with only smelly grooms to play with.' I wondered if he would ever see his beloved Rome again. If ever a youth was marked for misadventure - but he was off on another train of thought.

'Michele says that the prince admires his flagellation paintings of Christ and Saint Sebastian. I wonder why?' He gave a sly grin. 'Perhaps there will be something new- whips lying on the table next to the musical instruments?' I shuddered.

'I must go. Someone will be looking for me.'

'Never mind that.' He dragged me to the door. 'Let's visit Michele in the studio.' We made our way to a room in the eastern tower, not far from the prince's music room. I strained my ears for sounds but it was the siesta time. The studio was empty and the canvas was propped on an easel in front of the table. Covered with a Persian rug, the table held a couple of open scores, a lute, a wooden flute and a small violin, waiting for the six men who would stand behind it. Michele's paint-daubed smock lay on the floor nearby.

He had painted in the heads of some of the sitters. Gesualdo's long, thin face with its expression of frozen passion had been captured perfectly. I wondered whether Michele would paint that lop-sided, thin smile, but of course, people did not smile in portraits.

Cecco waved a hand at the painting. 'Ugly bastard, isn't he?'

'Don't disturb anything,' I chided. 'You know how Michele hates anything to be touched when he's working.'

'He doesn't mind anything I do,' said Cecco, full of bravado. Nevertheless, he carefully replaced the lute he was fiddling with in its correct position. Although I could see the colours of the velvet suits and the faces in my mind's eye, only Michele could transform the picture with light and darkness, giving new meaning to the images.

As if he read my thoughts Cecco said, 'In Rome they call

him Michele of the Shadows.' He wandered over to the stand where he had been grinding the paints for his master using blood-red cinnabar, linseed, coffee grounds and verdigris. He fingered the rabbit fur brushes and smiled at me.

'Have you come for instruction, or something else?' Michele's sarcastic voice accompanied the hard stare that he gave everyone he met -the look that saw through you, ready to transfer your essence onto canvas. We leapt in the air like guilty things as he stood in the doorway.

'We just came to admire, master,' Cecco said quickly. 'You don't mind, do you?' Michele gave the boy a friendly cuff and turned to me.

'I heard you were in trouble with the German hag. I warned you!' I shrugged and described the prince's intervention. Michele looked thoughtful. 'The great one has gone hunting to cool his temper. They treat me like a slave – me, the greatest artist in all Italy! They were supposed to sit for me today.'

He wandered around the room arranging things and fussing over the white linen shirt that one of the sitters would wear. As he moved he became more and more excited and angry. We often saw him fall into fits of fury without warning. He kept up a stream of abuse and obscenities, denouncing Gesualdo, all aristocrats, the school of Mannerism and the painters of Naples. 'This will give that asshole Lama something to think about.'

Giovan Battista Lama was the most famous Mannerist artist in the city. Michele referred to his paintings as "botched daubs." Cecco tried to soothe him, pouring a goblet of wine and saying that genius was never appreciated in its own time. He had heard someone say that.

When Michele had calmed down a little he began to work on the foreground of the painting. Cecco sidled out and I sat in a corner watching, fascinated, as always. He worked at astonishing speed before dropping the brush, running his paint spattered hands through his hair and coming over to sit next to me. We sat in silence for a moment, heads bowed. Looking up at each other we said as one 'what's wrong?' I laughed but Michele did not.

'You can begin,' he said. 'You've never really told me the full story about the murders. I want to see it all in my mind.' I looked around nervously. 'We shouldn't talk about it here, someone might be listening.'

He gave me that hard stare, 'No hope, no fear.' His eyes shone as he leaned forward. I began to speak rapidly and quietly, disturbed by his eagerness.

I described Donna Maria's chamber, the lovers in their bed with the duke wearing her embroidered nightgown. I recalled the ghastly red light from the torches that filled the room. As I recounted the details – the bed in shadow, the candles flickering, the screams, the blood and the clash of weapons, - Michele was transported. His eyes were fixed on something I could not see.

'Visions of the Damned!' he exclaimed. 'I can see it all. I wish I could paint the scene but the prince would not appreciate that.'

'But you were not there,' I protested.

'I can see it all in my mind,' he assured me, 'a place of shadows and blood-letting, like a crucifixion. Just my kind of subject. Perhaps I will paint it when I am in Malta.'

'Malta? Why are you going there? I thought you wanted to return to Rome.'

'I do, but it's impossible; I have bando capitale on my head. Anyone can kill me, cut off my head, send it back to Rome and be rewarded.' I shuddered and he patted my arm. 'The Knights of Malta want to commission a painting from me. They might even make me a Knight. I shall return to Naples and then leave for Valetta.'

'I shall miss you,' I whispered. 'You make me smile; you give me strength and courage.' This time he laughed his high-pitched laugh. '

'Not enough for you to fulfill your vow. The prince is still alive, even if not in good health. You have not done your work well, although I want him to survive long enough to pay me for the painting.'

It was true: the prince and Donna Leonora were always in poor health. Leonora had spent most the past year in Modena. She said she was only well when away from the castle. Her husband suffered constantly from attacks of breathlessness, stomach disorders, fatigue, and mysterious pains in the joints.

44

Farewells

Michele waved a paintbrush in the air and gave me a quizzical look.

'I know why they are both sick. Aurelia is still in the castle and she is poisoning both of them.' I stared at him for a long moment then I choked, laughing and crying together until I collapsed on the floor in a shaking heap. Michele looked at me in amazement.

'Have I said something amusing?' I shook my head. The gods were playing games with me again - or was it that goddess from the grove in Sicily?

'Are you telling me that she will succeed ...that my vow will never be fulfilled? He placed his hands on his hips and cocked his head to one side.

'I thought you had more sense, Laura. A man like the prince, a murderer, a sadist; there must be plenty of people who would like to kill him. There's the Carafa family for a start, not to mention his servants, his son, his daughter-in-law who plays with poisons; even the sainted Leonora, and probably anyone who has been forced to listen to his music for any length of time. He is hated wherever he goes.'

'But only Aurelia appears to be succeeding,' I sniffed. He shrugged and told me to move myself. 'Stop dithering and kill him if it's so important to you. No hope, no fear.'

He turned back to his canvas and studied it while I sat sniffing and thinking.

I knew about Gesualdo's former mistress, Aurelia d'Errico. The servants had told me all about her when I arrived. She had been cast off by her lover when he married Leonora. She was a self-confessed witch who had vowed to be revenged on her lover and his new wife. She had already been found guilty of attempted poisoning by the local bishop. The prince had wanted her hanged but the bishop had made a surprising decision. He ordered her to be imprisoned in her former lover's own castle. Perhaps the bishop had scores to settle with Gesualdo, as did everyone else.

'How can Aurelia harm anyone?' I spoke to Michele's back. 'She is locked in a cell, isn't she?' He laughed; 'She exercises a lot of influence nevertheless. The servants take food to her and she smuggles things out with their assistance. Cecco assures me of this.'

'Such as?'

'You had better ask them…but perhaps not. Watch more carefully when you are in the kitchen.' He turned and saw the look of despair on my face. 'Don't you see, this a perfect opportunity for you? Anything that happens to the prince now can be blamed on Aurelia.'

I went to Carnero for reassurance on this matter. He

always knew more about the prince's affairs than anyone. He told me something about Aurelia's trial and what the witnesses had said.

'They said that two small statues pierced by nails and with cords tied around their bodies had been found, together with a locket containing hair, nails of dead people, and other lascivious objects. These had been placed outside a castle door through which the prince often passed. Two iron pieces with some small lead coins had been found in a hole in the castle wall. It all looked very bad for Aurelia. The mystery is why she is still alive.'

I returned to my duties thinking about my potions and wondering what Aurelia was giving Gesualdo and his wife. I did not have long to wait. I came into the kitchen early one morning and found it empty. This was startling in itself. Then I saw there was one person crouching down in a shadowed corner mixing something in a small, wooden bowl set on a stool. It was Ugo Castelvietro, the prince's back-warmer. The youth looked healthier than of late. He leapt in the air when I came up to him, the picture of fright.

'That mixture looks as if it has turned to sludge,' I remarked, gazing down at the bowl. Was I mistaken or was there a faint, peculiar smell in the air? 'You have been stirring it for too long.' The youth jeered at me and whisked the bowl away.

'You are growing mazed in the head, old woman. This is no concern of yours.'

'Is it for Aurelia...or for the prince?' He swore at me, seized the bowl and left the kitchen swiftly. I returned thoughtfully to concocting a tisane. What was Castelvietro up to? I wondered what Gesualdo found so desirable about his favourite page, the skinny, dark little bastard with his almond-shaped eyes like an oriental.

It required a good deal of listening in to private conversations to get at the truth. I started to ignore remarks made to me, cultivating the idea that I was becoming deaf. People began to be careless in my presence, saying things they thought I could not overhear.

The pages were responsible: they were Aurelia's fetchers and carriers and no doubt she had ways of rewarding them, if not with money then in kind. She was still very beautiful, despite having endured torture in the bishop's prison.

I decided that the cook must be involved. He would have known that verjuice made from crab apples or sour grapes was ideal for concealing the taste of anything noxious, as was anything containing ginger or a rich egg sauce sharpened with a drop of lemon. The kitchen was as good as an alchemist's laboratory for experimenting with ingredients.

It was important to keep your wits about you in that kitchen. Donna Polissena and her German assistant tried out their poisons on the staff, especially any of the pages who had displeased her. Mostly they suffered mild stomach upsets. The Germans were not as skilled as the Italians in these matters. As it turned out, I was wrong about that.

One day I heard one of the pages whispering to another that he should place "something from our friend" in the dish that was to be served to the prince and his wife. The something appeared to be a slice of bread covered with a sauce. I thought that the poison must be in the sauce, but in that I was mistaken. There was still the matter of the mysterious soup that Castelvietro had been stirring. I needed to find out what it contained.

After dinner that evening the prince called for more wine and retired to his chamber, feeling unwell. Cecco, once again, solved the problem for me, his last favour before he left the castle.

He signalled to me that we should meet in our special place, the laundry room, where we would not be overheard. When I urged him to tell me what was being put in the prince's food he looked embarrassed - not his normal reaction.

'We...ell,' he lowered his voice. 'I heard this from the pages; make of it what you will.' I nodded.

'Yes?'

'They said that Aurelia put the bread into...into her woman's parts,' he blushed again, 'so that it was covered with her juices. Then it was served to the prince with a sauce covering the bread.' I gagged a little.

'What was in the soup that Castelvietro was stirring?' Cecco shrugged.

'I heard that it was an ordinary vegetable soup made by the cook. Aurelia gave Castelvietro something to add to it, something he carried in a tiny flask.' He opened his eyes wide. 'It was some of her menstrual blood.' We sat in shocked silence for a while. If such powerful witchcraft was being practiced on the prince and his wife, how had they survived so long? Donna Leonora might have been saved by her long absences but her husband was always at the castle.

What could I do? My vow was now unnecessary. I had left Venice and my child for this. I was worse than a fool. Something was very wrong, the curse was keeping me here, but for what, I did not know. I said nothing to Cecco and he went away to prepare for his journey. He would return to Rome when his master left for Malta.

Before he left the castle, I told Michele all my fears and he gave me strength, as always, in his cynical manner.

'Whatever you do, whatever happens, you must go back to Venice and find your daughter. You must do that just as I must get back to Rome somehow.' I sat slumped and miserable.

'I am afraid to do that, Michele. Everyone who comes close to me suffers or meets an untimely end. Perhaps it's better for my daughter if we never meet.' I put my head in my hands. Michele placed a hand on my shoulder.

'You don't really mean that, you know.'

'If only you were not leaving.' He shook his head and his paint-daubed hand touched my hair for a moment. I heard him mutter 'All my sins are mortal.' Then he stood up to leave. 'I must get ready. I can't stay here watching you snivel.'

Michele disliked farewells. When I came down to the kitchen next morning I found him already gone.

'Like a thief in the night,' the cook said. He had left a small package for me wrapped in a red cloth. Inside was a tiny painting of my head and shoulders wearing the dark blue silk shawl I had worn in *The Childhood of the Virgin.*

There was a note which I could just manage to read, 'To my St Anne from MM.'

I placed it in a box with my other treasure, Donna Maria's last remaining pearl.

45

Extract from the Journal of Carlo Gesualdo, Prince of Venosa

Undated

My wife's favourite brother, Cardinal Alessandro, is paying us a visit in a few days to offer his condolences on the death of our son. No doubt the real reason is to spy on me. He will learn nothing for I shall pay him every courtesy. A great banquet is being prepared in his honour.

Leonora has roused herself from her mourning to make ecstatic preparations. Roasted peacocks' tongues, of which I am very fond, will be served, as well as saffron pudding, the cardinal's favorite. My wife almost wept when she recounted this. She goes about the castle looking like a scrawny crow, although we are now out of mourning. It is fitting for a gentleman to wear black but a woman should always deck herself in bright silks and jewels. If a woman be not decorative of what use is she?

The Cardinal arrived this morning. He plans to stay for five days. I greeted him at the head of the grand staircase while

Leonora stood half way down. She and her brother greeted each other with much weeping and laughing and unseemly emotion. He accorded me the briefest of salutations, but I am accustomed to his extravagances. I know too much about him to be impressed with such behaviour.

I entertained him royally at the first banquet with all manner of delicacies and wines. Leonora announced that she intends to remain in mourning for the rest of her life. The Cardinal nodded approvingly. Naturally, this destroyed all light conversation at the table. Northerners have no sense of the fitness of things.

The Cardinal spoke eloquently of the rigours of his journey from Rome, including a ferocious storm at sea. He mentioned a visit to Donna Ippolita, Princess of Mirandola, his sister and thus my sister-in-law. I have so far avoided a visit from any more of Leonora's relatives.

The musical entertainment was provided by that exquisite trio, the Ladies of Ferrara. The guests were delighted and many expressed themselves in the usual Neapolitan manner – pretending to stab themselves, so overcome were they by the singing. Our northern guests appeared somewhat bemused.

In short, the visit was a success although a strain on my purse. I showed the Cardinal the picture in the chapel of Santa Maria and asked his opinion of it, but he merely said that the building of the chapel would obtain many heavenly blessings for me. He avoided my eyes as he said this. Of course, they all think I am damned…and perhaps they are right. Mea culpa.

46

Venison and Saffron Pudding

We heard that Donna Leonora's brother was expected at the castle, the notorious Cardinal. I remember that visit well. The prince's back warmer Ugo Castelvietro, was suddenly promoted to be his official food taster. Gesualdo's health was worse than ever and he was convinced that he was being poisoned. I heard him say to Ugo, 'You must safeguard my life.' The page's life was, naturally, of no account. The prince gave the usual litany of his ailments, 'stomach pains, aching joints, insomnia, pains in the head and breathlessness.' Ugo's face was a picture.

The Cardinal brought his own food taster, as would anyone visiting Don Gesualdo, a man with an appetite for murder and a strong dislike of his wife's relatives. It was a problem because so many people wished the prince dead.

The castle cook at that time was a man of great skill called Giovanni Silvero. He could produce the most succulent kid or venison, the tastiest capons and fennel sausages. I would have died to taste those sausages. They would make the angels salivate. He was equally skilled with sugar confections - the equal of the cooks in Palermo.

A splendid banquet was prepared including almonds dipped in melted sugar and covered with gold leaf. Carnero stole one for me. It was the food of heaven. There was also his fricassee of song bird covered in a magical spiced sauce. The kitchen became unbearable to the servants while all this was cooking. The smells were such that we could scarcely control ourselves.

The day before the Cardinal was expected I found a strange fellow in the kitchen corner. He was a short, whey-faced Genoese who was passing the time by tormenting the steward's cat, a tabby with one eye. Dio mio! How the steward loved that cat. Carnero whispered to me,

'If the steward catches this arsehole molesting his pet he will run him through and display his skinny arse on the castle turrets.'

The cook said, 'He is the Cardinal's food taster.' He beckoned the man over and the creature drew himself up in a self-important manner.

'His Eminence will not touch liver of any kind even if it is steeped in wine and sweetened with honey. He does, however, love sugar fancies of every kind.

'He loves sugar, you say?' sneered the cook. 'And he has the teeth to prove it!' We laughed as the food taster scowled and returned to his corner. Of course, it was no laughing matter to Castelvietro. As the cook recited the list of ingredients for the banquet, the page grew more agitated by the minute. The Cardinal's food taster was also listening intently; his sticking out ears grew red with the effort of concentration. Carnero and I consulted together on the outcome.

'It's quite possible that the Cardinal might try to arrange Gesualdo's death to please his beloved sister. They are very close - suspiciously close, it's rumoured.' I replied that it would probably be Ugo who would die.

'The prince will live to compose another madrigal to torment us.'

The cook Giovanni is trustworthy. He has nothing to gain by poisoning anyone. That left almost a hundred others in the castle who might be tempted, from musicians to pot boys.

A message came that the cardinal's entourage had been sighted outside the town. The cook told Ugo to put his head in the water butt and 'liven up.' The page went to put on his velvet jerkin looking like death.

Of course, we contrived to watch everything from behind pillars. Cardinal Alessandro walked up the grand staircase enveloped in rustling red satin. His gloves were perfumed with attar of roses like a whore's. Gesualdo was at the top of the stairs, expressionless, and dressed in black as always.

Donna Leonora stood half way up the stairs. She was so excited and tearful I thought she would topple over. She had donned a gown of black satin with a quilted hem and a jewel-encrusted white lace collar - a change from her usual black velvet.

I slipped back to the kitchen to assist the cook. I could hear the prince's musicians singing one of his madrigals, *Moro, Lasso*. As I entered the hall I saw that the composer's eyes were closed in ecstasy. The cardinal looked pained and turned to his sister for support. *"Mercy! I cry as I weep but who listens?"* sang the choir.

They could have been echoing the feelings of many of us, especially Ugo's.

Gesualdo opened his eyes and pushed the wine goblet towards the page. 'Drink!' Ugo went a faint green colour and gulped a mouthful. He closed his eyes and tottered slightly. Gesualdo raised the goblet to his brother-in-law and they drank a polite toast, the little Genoese having tasted the Cardinal's wine. Platters of food were carried in while Giovanni oversaw everything, shouting and waving, exhorting the servants to take care.

A huge swan was the centrepiece of the table surrounded by lilies which appear on the prince's coat of arms. I watched again as Ugo tasted some veal and peacock's tongue. Then a platter of meatballs was carried in which had been liberally laced with coriander and ginger.

How thoughtful of Giovanni to please the host and his guest in this way. Coriander is a cure for impotency- ideal for Gesualdo, although the beatings are more effective. As for ginger, it provokes lust, although, if the rumours about the cardinal are correct he has little need of it. A hot spice like ginger could mask the taste of various unpleasant and potentially fatal ingredients – a problem for Ugo.

The three ladies from Ferrara who are famous for their singing performed at this point. The prince had persuaded them to return south with him much to the disgust of the court at Ferrara. The Cardinal registered his disapproval by talking loudly throughout the performance, describing the terrors of the storm he encountered on his journey.

Gesualdo looked furious. Interrupting music and song

was unpardonable as far as he was concerned. He picked at his food, looking like a thundercloud as he prepared to do battle with the cardinal. The cook beckoned to me and slipped a twist of paper into my hand.

'Give this to Ugo when the guests are not looking. It is unicorn powder – a sovereign remedy against poison.' I do not know how the cook obtained this powder. Perhaps he stole it from the prince's chamber.

I passed the powder to Ugo just as Gesualdo called for his favourite eels in tomato sauce. He called to his page to taste these as well as a bowl of salad. A sudden hush fell as the guests watched and the little Genoese smirked. We all expected the worst, but Ugo slipped the powder into his mouth before tasting the eels. Poor boy; I disliked the little shit but he was only fifteen. Why should he die?

Well, he swallowed a little of the eels and remained upright. Either they were not poisoned after all, or we should all start praying to unicorns

There remained only the dessert. The saffron pudding was prominently displayed. Everyone paused to consider Giovanni's delicate concoction. Heavenly aromas of cinnamon and cloves and honey filled the air, transporting me once again to my Sicilian youth. When Gesualdo tasted the pudding he suddenly dropped his silver spoon and screamed, waving his arm angrily at the musicians. They had played a wrong note, naturally. I think he would cheerfully have ordered the execution of them all at that moment.

I retreated back to the kitchen where the cook was pouring water and wine down Ugo's throat. He had an idea, he told us. He would take the little Genoese to see Aurelia. Between them they would convince him that he would have a much better life as Gesualdo's food taster – with extra benefits, as it were. The prince could be convinced that he should not endanger the life of his favourite back warmer any more. The chance to spite the cardinal would also please him.

Everything went according to plan. The cardinal did not notice his food taster's absence from the entourage. He was anxious to leave as soon as possible. No doubt he recruited another one in the next town. I only wish Michele had been there to witness it all.

That is how it was at the castle.

Unfortunately for the Genoese, Aurelia was about to be dispatched. The prince had petitioned the Vatican to overrule the local bishop who had decreed that she should be imprisoned in the castle. She was finally removed from her cell in chains and loaded onto a cart to be sent to Naples and the Viceroy's prison.

She screamed horribly, calling down curses on the prince and his family and the entire household. It was whispered that many of the servants wet themselves with fear. Meanwhile, her former lover shut himself in his music room where five singers performed one of his madrigals, *T'amo Mia Vita*, singing and playing loudly in an attempt to drown out the witch's cries.

Donna Leonora had once again departed for Modena for an extended stay. She would remain there until her husband's threats dragged her back. She will be relieved to know that Aurelia has left the castle.

The prince looked worse than ever: haggard and stick thin, short of breath and complaining, as always, of chronic aches and pains. I decided to prepare one of my special tisanes for him. The beatings by his pages increased in number. The lives of those youths were full of amusement. Not only did they have the pleasure of beating their master daily, but they had also enjoyed Aurelia's favours. They did not know that she was exhibiting signs of the French sickness. If they had they might have run screaming from the castle.

When I first returned to Naples from Venice and I was employed at the Hospital for the Incurables in the city, fully three quarters of the unfortunates in that place were suffering from the Great Pox. This foul disease had been brought to Naples from the New World. It was said that French soldiers carried it when they invaded the city a hundred years ago. They were soon gone but within a year the pox made its appearance on the faces of the local whores and their clients. It became known as the French disease, the curse of Venus and other less polite names.

The disease spared no-one from cardinals and princes to the soldiery and the lowliest beggar. Terrible pustules appeared all over the body starting in the private parts. These gave off a stench so terrible that we feared to be near the sufferers. Sometimes the victims appeared to be given a pardon by God and remained a while unaffected, but the affliction would return unabated leaving them howling like dogs with their flesh coming off their bones until death delivered them from their agony. Sometimes, the silver tincture called mercury was administered to victims, if they had money. It caused their faces to turn grey-blue.

Aurelia's face was largely unaffected when I saw her in her cell, but I knew the signs that might have escaped the pages. She had begun to cover herself to hide them and no doubt she tried to doctor herself with her knowledge of the black arts, but she did not fool me. I wondered if she had passed the disease to the prince.

After Aurelia's departure Gesualdo was more troubled than ever. He was closeted n his tower room with his books and music for long hours. It was rumoured that he was practicing the black arts.

47

Extract from the Journal of
Carlo Gesualdo, Prince of Venosa

October 20.1610

I am in correspondence with Giambattista Della Porta regarding matters alchemical, I have followed the work of this master of science for some years and I did not lose faith in him during the period when his writings were suppressed by the Inquisition.

My particular reason for consulting him on this occasion was my acquisition of an amulet, possibly from ancient Greece. It was found in Sicily near Ortigia and sold to me by a merchant in Naples. I have attempted to decipher the symbols on the amulet without success. It is a small disc in bronze and I have discovered that the writing on it is not Greek but possibly from an earlier lost civilization. I have consulted antique books without success. Surely Della Porta will have the arcane knowledge necessary to solve this mystery.

I feel in my bones that the amulet can offer some kind of protection or charm against demons. If I could unlock its secrets

I would be in a powerful position, safe from the forces of darkness that surround me in this place.

October 30

Della Porta has established that the amulet comes from the island of Crete where, according to legend, the Minotaur lurked in its labyrinth. I fear there is little chance of deciphering something of such antiquity.

He suggests that such objects can be understood through natural magic. He believes that certain ancient artifacts may be charged or impregnated with a spell, a charm, or even a curse that will follow their owners through the ages. If the correct formula can be discovered, the secret can be unlocked. This is my task and it is proving a difficult one.

I have consulted many books in the library at Venosa without success. Precious hours of composing and playing have been sacrificed in this task, but I am as one possessed. Sometimes I feel I am already in the grip of some nameless enchantment emanating from the amulet. Can its influence be so strong?

For many nights now I have been unable to sleep. My eyes start from my head and I am like a somnambulist, a sleepwalker, by day as well as by night. My family has noticed my haggard appearance although without expressing any great concern. Leonora, lately returned unexpectedly from Modena, has noticed that I frequently leave my bed at night. She has told everyone that I am a sleepwalker. No doubt the servants are greatly amused.

Last night I made my way onto the castle ramparts at midnight. I ran aimlessly to and fro clutching the amulet in my hand. One moment the sky was bright with starlight and a half moon, the next instant the moon became full of blood. I gave a cry and almost hurled the amulet into the courtyard below. I have no recollection of returning to my bed but I awoke there this morning after dreaming of insubstantial, shadowy yet menacing things.

November 12

Following more advice from Della Porta I have placed the amulet in the music room and I shall play my compositions to it. The sound waves moving through the air may unlock its secrets by natural magic.

Yesterday I played on the archlute and the cembalo after placing the amulet on a table close by. I played two sprightly madrigals, "All'ombra degli Allori" and, "Donna se m'ancidete" written for the three divine sopranos from Ferrara. I noticed that as I played these ravishing harmonies the atmosphere in the room began to change as if air was rushing through rapidly. I was greatly encouraged by this and proceeded to play "Morro Lasso" with its sudden dissonances. To my horror I felt the violent climaxes and significant pauses in this piece causing a sharp rise in what I must call the audient menace in the air. Della Porta was right; I have unlocked some power from the amulet but I fear it is entirely negative.

I hurried from the room and did not return until evening when I stood by the window looking out over the countryside. The moon resembled a giant bruise. I was again aware of a change in the air in the chamber and a strange whistling noise, faint and high-pitched – a note so strange that it might have been produced by Victorino's amazing archicembalo.

I turned around, dreading what I might see, but the chamber was empty and the amulet still in its place. I left the room, feeling faint with my limbs shaking. After a while I returned and everything appeared normal. The serving maid who seems familiar to me brought herbal tea. She looked at me strangely, I thought, as she left the room. Her presence makes me uneasy although I cannot say why. After I drank I sought my bed and slept deeply for a few hours, but my dreams were strange and terrible.

A calamity occurred last night that has caused great fear and dread among us all. One of the young serving wenches came into the music room during my absence, perhaps thinking to sweep or dust. A few moments later terrible screams were heard and the wench's body was found at the foot of the great staircase. Her injuries were terrible to behold and there is now much murmuring among the staff.

Later, Don Emanuele made an unexpected appearance in the great hall urging me to desist from whatever unholy occupation I was engaged in. Those were his words. I reproached him for his lack of respect but he marched angrily from my presence, as always. I inspected the amulet anxiously and I felt vibrations coming from it such as would be given out by a large musical instrument after it has been played.

My steward declared that the dead girl, Bianca, was so grievously injured that it was as if she had been hurled from the top of the staircase with great force. I shall have to pay some compensation to her family.

I have written again to Della Porta telling him of my fears.

Surely, he must understand these midnight matters. He responded with a theory that the amulet may require a sacrifice in the same way that new buildings must have an offering in the form of a human being or an animal sealed into the brickwork.

I remain uneasy and this morning I removed the amulet to an unused room where I sealed it in a strong casket. These measures have lifted the charged atmosphere in the music room somewhat, but there is a miasma of melancholy and something worse within the castle that is felt by everyone.

Several more servants left my service this morning and the steward must go further afield to find more. Leonora is already whining about returning to Modena for another extended visit. Naturally, I have refused this request. There is always the possibility that she may be chosen as another sacrifice, thus ridding me of one more aggravation. Ha! I jest, but only a little.

Emanuele has returned again to Venosa while his bitch of a wife weaves her web of deceit in every corner, aided by her German assistant. Women are, as always, a curse on this house.

November 20

I wrote again to Della Porta urging him in the strongest terms to visit me so that we may consult together and he can examine the amulet. I now feel the greatest reluctance in handling the object.

November 24

Della Porta has sent me a long letter. He is reluctant to leave Naples being absorbed in various experiments. He complains that the fame of Galileo will overshadow his own achievements.

As an afterthought, he gave me his opinion that my music may have released some kind of elemental – a thing so powerful that it destroys indiscriminately. He commends me to seek the help of the Church.

I retired to bed early feeling overcome almost to death.

I have summoned my physician who is treating me with dried, powdered fox lung which he says is a sovereign cure for my breathlessness. We shall see.

48

The Devil's Tune

Who knew what devilry the prince was concocting up in his tower room? The death of poor Bianca terrified everyone. She was a sweet girl, newly arrived from the countryside near Avellino. I do not know what possessed her to enter the prince's music room to clean. We all had strict instructions not to enter the room unless he sent for us. Perhaps something evil lured her there.

Carnero saw the body. She had been covered over by the time I arrived on the scene. I saw only a blood-soaked sheet before they carried her away. He said her injuries were terrible. He agrees with the steward that she must have been thrown from the top of the staircase. The cook claimed that it was Aurelia weaving her spells from afar, but the idea was laughable. That woman had very little skill other than in poisons.

I drew Carnero aside and asked him what should be done.

'You know what needs to be done, Laura. The prince must be killed. It should have been done years ago.' I stood with my back against the courtyard wall to stiffen my spine and my courage. Carnero went on, 'give him one of your potions. He is taking so many medicines nobody will know what harmed him.'

I swallowed hard; 'nothing he takes appears to work. He is a hard man to kill.' I was making excuses of course, but the prince did, indeed, appear to be indestructible. He was one of those people who are always ailing, always fragile, but long-lived.

Carnero waved a crooked arm in front of my face. 'I will help you, Laura. I will give the drink to him myself if you are afraid. If we do nothing one of us could be lying at the foot of the staircase next time. We have little to lose He could destroy us all with his occult meddling.'

'My daughter…' I heard myself whisper, 'I must live for my daughter.'

'Let me think about it,' I told him. 'It must be something that will not fail this time.' He nodded and patted my hand and we parted.

The prince appeared at dinner that night for the first time in a week. His usually immaculate, black-clad figure showed signs of inattention. The ruff was slightly askew, the velvet jerkin a little dusty. He no longer had a valet; Bardotti had not been replaced. The pages were supposed to attend to all his needs but both they and their master were in such a state of fear and trembling that such things as personal toilettes were no longer important.

Gesualdo was no coward; he was fearless on horseback and had studied the arts of war, but the fear of demons is universal and there is no defence against it. The Prince of Venosa now resembled a sick bird and his wife was spending all her time on her knees in the chapel. He had just enough strength left to forbid her to return to Modena. I went into the kitchen to see what the cook had prepared for the meal.

'Our master has little appetite,' said Giovanni. He had prepared some spit-roasted songbirds with a spicy sauce, 'But perhaps I should have obtained his favourite eels?' I thought it made little difference. The prince did not look as if food was on his mind. I sat in a corner chewing on a piece of bread and thinking. Castelvietro was agitating about the place terrified out of his wits.

'He is convinced he is to be the next victim of the witchery in the castle,' said Giovanni. 'He has the brains of a chicken.' I said nothing but I had often seen the cook pulling the wishbone of a chicken and consulting its entrails.

To make matters worse a strong wind had got up – "a devil's wind," according to Donna Polissena's German assistant. It began to rain heavily and the old castle with its draughts and ancient stone walls became dank and chilly. The wind verily whistled around corners and down stairways causing everyone to jump out of their skins. I worked alone in Donna Polissena's chamber trying to decide on a concoction for the prince while wishing that he had caught the French Pox or might be cursed with boils like one of the plagues of Egypt.

When I left the chamber, carrying linen to be washed, I met Castelvietro hurrying along the passage looking over his shoulder from time to time as if afraid of his own shadow.

'What is it?' I asked him. His left eye twitched as he clutched my apron.

'I know now for sure that the master is in league with the devil.'

'How?' The page gave a triumphant grin. 'I recollected this morning that I had never heard the prince fart.' Truly the entire castle and its inmates were bewitched. From the tower room I heard the faint strains of a piece of music the prince was writing for the church, *Woe is me O Lord because I have sinned greatly in my life.* Amen to that I told myself.

I could not decide on the best poison for my purpose. Whenever I tried to think about the problem my mind became fogged and sluggish. In my heart, I knew I did not want to do this thing, in spite of my vow to Donna Maria, despite my hatred for him. I was happy to give him tisanes that would make him vomit or weaken him, but a strong poison that would kill outright was another matter. When I poisoned Aldo Pretti I had been full of fury - and younger, more hot-headed. The thought of my daughter nagged at me, squeezed my heart and turned my innards to water. What would she think if she knew what I had done, not once but more than once? Surely, she would run from me in horror if we ever found each other?

Carnero understood me too well. He knew I was reluctant to act. He took pity on me and consulted a sorcerer in a nearby village. The powder he obtained was infallible, according to the sorcerer. Heaven knows what the powder contained. Carnero muttered about aborted foetuses and a toad. There was always a toad in these cases.

'I am too conspicuous,' Carnero said. 'You must put the powder in his wine. It will give him a fever or another one of his attacks. No-one will suspect anything.'

If only life always went according to plan. "No hope, no fear," I told myself as I slipped the powder into the carafe of wine placed on a tray by the pages. ' I suppose I absolved myself this time because I had not actually prepared the potion. It rested on the kitchen table while they chatted amongst themselves. Giovanni's back was turned and the steward was occupied with his accounts. Unable to bear the suspense, I left the room.

Carnero came to find me some time later. 'You had better see this,' was all he said. I followed him, my spine rigid with fear. The kitchen was full of people talking and gesticulating. The sound of weeping came from a corner. Holy Mother!

The steward's cat had knocked the carafe over. Wine spilled across the floor and the cat, which would eat or drink anything, had lapped at it. Its bloated corpse was stretched out on the floor already rigid. The steward was inconsolable,

Carnero raised his eyebrows and whispered, 'That cat has cost me five ducats.'

Later I could see that it was almost laughable, although not for the cat. Did it not prove that feeble, ailing Gesualdo was indestructible?

'Perhaps it is his music that preserves him,' Carnero remarked when we were alone. ' It must have some kind of protective effect like magical aspic.' He laughed and wriggled his twisted body. 'There is always tomorrow.'

49

No Hope: No Fear

July 6.1609

Michele came back to Naples. I do not know how he managed to send me a message but he had his own methods. A small boy, the son of one of the grooms, came to me in the kitchen and told me that I should go at once to the stables.

'What am I wanted for?' The boy shrugged and tugged at my skirt.

'Come now, be quick, someone's waiting.'

At the stables, I found a shifty looking, dust-covered man who was completely unknown to me. He whispered in my ear, his garlic-laden breath mingling in my nostrils with the steaming breath of the horses.

Michele had been in Malta this past year painting for the Knights who had made him one of their own. I smiled to think of him as Sire Michelangelo Merisi. He had been given a gold chain and two black slaves as a mark of the esteem in which he was held by the Grand Master, Alof de Wignacourt, but he had thrown it all away by brawling, drunkenness and insulting another knight. He had been thrown into prison but had escaped to Sicily where he was offered a number of commissions. Now he was back in Naples and in trouble.

'Big trouble,' said the man over his shoulder, before walking away.

I begged permission to go into the city for family reasons. Nobody knew that I had no relatives there, except Carnero. As Donna Polissena was on a religious retreat away from the castle, I was allowed to set off in the wine merchant's cart. I found Michele in a cheap lodging house in a terrible state. He was shaking with ague and as yellow as Fillide's canary.

I could see that he was suffering from marsh fever. I prepared some herbal medicine for him distilled from fenugreek root sweetened with honey which he hated. I held his nose and poured the liquid down his throat.

'You can't do this to me,' he spluttered. 'Don't you know that I am a Knight of Malta?'

'You **were** a Knight,' I reminded him. 'Now they want your head.' He shrugged and swallowed some wine to take away the taste.

'Everyone tries to kill me eventually – even you with your potions.' I ignored his moans and warned him to take better care of himself but he was not listening: already he was drinking strong wine stagger around the room trying to watch for his enemies and complaining constantly. 'The list of my enemies is so long it would be easier to think of a group that did **not** want my head.'

The Knights, of course, had a score to settle with him, but the Vatican had been on his trail since he left Rome as well as the family of the man he had killed in a brawl. Perhaps the Inquisition was also on his trail. The Jesuits had torn down his paintings in churches, declaring them to be blasphemous.

'Yes, the Jesuits loath me - it's mutual, of course.' I nodded agreement; our shared hatred of that organization was another bond between us.

'I would die happy if I could stick my knife in one of them.' His mouth twisted in a savage grin. 'I do not give two farts for the Church.'

After that visit, I had to return to the castle so I was not around when he re-visited the Cherry Tavern in search of alcoholic oblivion or some cheap whores. Some time passed before the messenger came back to tell me that Michele was at the convent of St Ursula. He had been attacked by five men in the tavern and was seriously injured.

'They say he won't live.' The messenger nodded and walked away again.

When I managed to reach the city, I would not have recognized the man who lay in the narrow bed, naked except for a soiled sheet over his lower limbs. A sword thrust had split his face from the left eyebrow to the chin. The wound had been crudely sewn up, probably by a horse doctor. The skin had been pulled and stretched so much that he could barely speak through his twisted mouth. The rest of his face was a mass of purple and yellow flesh with dried blood caked around the nostrils. The nuns told me that he had lost most of his teeth. Sweat poured off him and the stench was gross.

I bent over him and wept a little. He opened his eyes and

I think he knew me although he was full of the poppy juice the nuns had given him to dull the pain. He managed to whisper one word, 'Shit!' before fainting.

I realized that would be no escape for Michele. His enemies were intent on his destruction. How could they do this to the greatest artist in Christendom?

He was a sick man for almost a year, suffering one fever after another. Herbal remedies were given to him daily and eventually he managed to get up and resume painting. The nuns were pleased to have the famous artist under their roof and he painted a *Martyrdom of St Ursula* for the father of one of the novices.

When he was strong enough he returned to the Colonna palace in Chiaia at the request of his patron. Nobody knew that he was completing the last pictures he would ever paint. I refused to pose for him again even in the darkest of backgrounds.

'Why not?' he asked.

'I will bring you more bad luck. It follows me everywhere.' I knew how ridiculous that sounded. Nobody could have worse luck than Michele at that moment.

His mood remained grim. It was only when a messenger arrived with the news that the Pope was, after all, considering a pardon for him that the depression lifted. The expression on his twisted face might almost have been joyful. I had not fully realized how much he longed to return to Rome. It was the one place where he felt at home, where he could swim easily in its currents.

'I am only truly alive in Rome,' he said apologetically, unable to look me in the eye. How could he trust the word of the Vatican after everything that had happened to him? Yet he was determined to leave at the earliest opportunity.

'You are not fully recovered,' I told him as he bade me a fond farewell. His skinny frame in its crumpled velvet suit was twitching with anticipation as the felucca arrived. He stepped into the boat clutching his canvases under his arm. The rowers dipped their oars and pulled away from the quay. He did not look back.

One of the paintings he carried was *David with the Head of Goliath*, his very last work. On to the face of Goliath he had painted his own features as they were before the disfigurement; his hooded eyes glaring out at the world with that hard stare the Spanish call the mirada fuerte.

I never saw him again. Weeks later I heard of his death on a lonely beach in Tuscany – Porto Ercole, they said. Whether he drowned or died of a fever or was assassinated, I do not know. He was probably betrayed.

By the time he left Naples he was hideous to look upon and more and more withdrawn, but I loved him as a brother. I can't explain why. We were friends, not lovers, but each of us had need of a special friend.

I recognized in him another lost soul, someone who also carried a curse. We were both killers after all, but he was also a genius and that is a curse of a different kind. Now there was nothing left for me except to fulfill my vow – no hope, no fear.

I lay awake that night in the tiny room I shared with another servant. The news of Michele's death had arrived earlier. I stared out through the small window at a gibbous moon. As always, I saw the familiar figures there - Donna Maria, Fillide, Sarah, Gaetano and now a fifth figure, Michele. My only comfort was that there was no figure representing my daughter. I took this to mean that she still lived and I would find her one day

50

Extract from the Journal of
Carlo Gesualdo, Prince of Venosa

July16.1609

When I visited the chapel of Santa Maria delle Grazie this morning I found my wife studying the altarpiece intently. She started like a guilty thing when I spoke to her and her expression was not welcoming. I believe she is trying to interpret the picture in such a way as to create more scandal with her precious brothers. She corresponds with them ceaselessly now that she has returned from Modena.

The artist Giovan Battista Lama painted the altarpiece. It depicts my sainted uncle San Carlo Borromeo presenting me to the Holy Redeemer in penitence. A host of saintly characters inhabit the canvas pointing at me as a penitent sinner. The Redeemer's hand is raised in a gesture of absolution. At the bottom of the canvas, engulfed in the flames of Purgatory are the figures of my late wife and her lover with angels.

When I asked for her opinion of the work she looked discomforted and muttered that it was well enough, "although the canvas is somewhat crowded." Now she is an expert on art as well as music. I told her that her beloved brother the cardinal thought well of it. At this her expression became inscrutable.

.

51

The Years

The prince lived for another four years and I... I was trapped there, stuck like a fly in syrup while life at the castle became more unbearable daily.

I brooded more and more on my daughter and her fate. The sound of a child's laughter in the castle tormented me, although I knew that my child was now grown. All those years had passed and I had missed them. These thoughts were so unbearable that I tried to make my mind blank –to think of something, anything else.

Soon after I heard of Michele's death the prince tried to lift the gloom by staging a pageant. There would be a palio; a horse race and a battle axe competition. Of course, there was more involved than simply a desire to cheer up the castle's inhabitants. After the terrible death of the maid, Bianca, the prince became more disordered in his mind and his health grew steadily worse without any help from me.

Life was quieter now that Aurelia had been dispatched from the castle but Donna Polissena was still experimenting with her potions. Donna Leonora had gone to Modena once more and her husband, despite his dessicated appearance and poor health, had taken yet another mistress. Her name was Serafina and she was one of Donna Leonora's ladies- in-waiting. The prince ordered Serafina to stay behind when his wife travelled north to tell her troubles to her brothers. She would take Donna Leonora's place at the pageant in which we would all take part. I was to be a herald wearing a ridiculous hat and carrying a long scroll.

Carnero urged me to make a wager –"a certainty to win" in the palio. He persuaded me to back a magnificent chestnut. It came second from last.

Don Emanuele's behaviour, meanwhile, was becoming wilder and more outrageous. He did everything possible to enrage his father including taking up with Rosalia Melli, the prince's original mistress and the mother of his bastard son Don Antonio. When Antonio had found his mother and his half-brother in bed together Don Emanuele had mocked him for "a bastard fool." The youth rushed to find his sword and there could have been a repeat of the original murders in another bedchamber if Don Antonio had not been restrained.

Not content with that insult, Don Emanuele had also managed to bed Serafina. If his father knew that he gave no sign. I was tortured with fear of what might happen to Donna Maria's son. He was not a pleasant person, I had to admit. He had his mother's blonde beauty but he was arrogant and insolent. I blamed the prince for this. With such a father how could the son of a murdered mother be anything else?

The servants knew that Don Emanuele's arguments with his father had grown more frequent in recent months. The anguished, tortured notes of the prince's music often rose in to the air accompanied by shouts from the two men and occasional shrieks from Donna Polissena. The son took what revenge he could. Helping himself to his father's mistress, however, might be a step too far.

On quieter days when the prince was not in the music room I would creep in to admire Michele's painting which hung in splendour against the white walls. Everyone had been summoned to admire it. The faces were unforgettable, the handsome face of Don Antonio, the suave Don Ettore and Prince Carlo Gesualdo as we all knew him – the long thin white face, the opaque black eyes and the black beard miraculously untouched by grey. I thought of my own streaked locks and resolved to rub walnut oil into them to make them dark again. Don Emanuele had either refused to pose for the portrait or had not been invited.

The rich colours of the velvets glowed from the canvas. So life-like was the scene that one of the servants tried to lift the lute from the picture and was soundly beaten for his mistake. The prince had been so pleased with the painting that he had paid immediately – a thing unheard of. Now Michele was gone forever and the mad composer serenaded the painting every day.

Hundreds of people attended the pageant from the surrounding area and there was much feasting and merrymaking. The prince's party looked tense and uneasy. The rest of us were agog with anticipation. The highlight of the pageant was the battle axe competition between Don Emanuele and Don Antonio.

The two contestants held up their shields and began to wield the axes, but this appeared to be no more than a ritual. Soon, they abandoned the axes and took up swords and daggers, using their cloaks as bucklers. They were well-matched as they lunged and parried, uttering oaths through clenched teeth.

Don Emanuele gave a sudden lunge and inflicted a wound in his half -brother's sword arm. Don Antonio dropped his sword and rolled over on the ground while onlookers gasped and groaned at the popular young man's plight. He quickly recovered and came at Don Emanuele with a snarl cutting him on the shoulder.

Who knows what would have happened if their father had not halted the fight? Suddenly, Don Emanuele turned towards the dais and triumphantly produced Serafina's white scarf from his doublet. He waved it at the audience as she blushed and looked uneasily at the prince who remained inscrutable, wrapped in his long black cloak on this warm day. Later, I heard that Serafina was not summoned to the prince's bed that night. Castelvietro took her place.

After the pageant, an eerie silence settled over the castle. Physicians were summoned to Gesualdo, who was suffering another attack of breathlessness, Don Emanuele left for Venosa once more and Don Antonio returned to Naples. As for Serafina, she did not remain long at the castle.

When I was alone or working in Donna Polissena's chamber my thoughts would turn again to my daughter.

What would she think if she could see this grey haired, worn creature who had abandoned her? The thought was like a knife in my entrails.

52

Letter from the
Prince of Venosa to Della Porta

I thank you for sending me the formula for Veninum Lupinum. A person from the village who is indebted to me had the ingredients made up as you instructed – a concoction of aconite, taxus, caustic lime, arsenic, bitter almonds and powdered glass, mixed with honey and raisins made into small balls resembling sweetmeats.

I have sent them in a casket to my mistress. I trust she will bother me no more. The concoction is a strong poison, as you advised. If I did not allow my wife to cuckold me still less will I allow my mistress to do so.

53

Black Hearts and Black Velvet

We heard of the fate of Serafina. Carnero was commanded by the prince to deliver a box of poisoned sweetmeats to the girl. The poor dwarf was in tears when he told me.

'I was her executioner, Laura. If only I had known.' I comforted him as best I could. Aristocrats cared nothing for the lives of ordinary people. And who would avenge Serafina? That is how it was in the household of Gesualdo.

One of my abiding memories is of the bales of black velvet that flowed into the castle every year, like a river of darkness, to provide the clothing for the prince and princess, who wore no other colour. Donna Leonora had chosen to remain in mourning perpetually and I had never seen the prince in anything but Spanish black except at his wedding to Donna Maria.

I remember then that he wore a doublet of russet silk lined with linen with matching breeches decorated with ribbons. Diamonds had winked at his neck and in his ears, but soon he would resort to funereal hues. For a while there was also a supply of pink velvet delivered secretly for the witch-whore Aurelia, who was very fond of the colour during the years when she was still in favour. After her imprisonment Gesualdo would no longer pay for anything, but she continued to wear the same pink gown, trimmed with gold lace – bedraggled finery for a tarnished creature.

But the colours of Michele's painting were finer than anything the silk weavers of Florence could produce and they remained to remind me of him in the narrow, vaulted music room.

My employer, Donna Polissena and her German assistant were always watching everything, inciting, whispering with the pages, creating tension and ill-will wherever they could. Carnero watched too; we both watched and listened but my friend knew that the prince was tiring of him and he would soon be pensioned off. Then I would have no friend at all within those walls.

'I will not go far, Laura,' he promised me. 'I will take rooms in the village and you may visit me whenever you are able.' Gesualdo tired of everyone eventually, especially his wife and daughter-in-law. His relations with his son remained as turbulent as ever.

And the music…always the music pouring out of that tower room in notes shrill with guilt and discordant with desperation; music for the church from his black soul, entreating the Almighty for forgiveness.

His new madrigal *Resta di Darmi Noia* ended with the words "For me all joy is dead, nor can I hope ever again to find happiness." I hoped the shadow of my dead mistress could hear those words and rejoice in them.

Although Donna Polisenna and her assistant concocted poisons in secret, they were less inclined to labour over ingredients required for other things. I spent hours pounding and grinding silver and pearl and other fine materials, blending them with almond oil, musk, ambergris, even mother's milk, into the finest creams that my employer used to preserve her pale complexion. She was very proud of her milky, unblemished skin and no expense was spared to enhance it.

'I vant the skin of a fifteen- year- old,' she declared in her strange accent. Already, her face was less blooming than it had been when I first arrived at the castle. Displeased with her pale eyebrows, she used mink pieces that were attached to her skin with egg white.

I met with Carnero whenever I had the opportunity. Sometimes we reminisced about our childhood. I told him about my time in Sicily, although I could not bring myself to mention the peddler.

Carnero told me of his sad childhood. 'When I was born my mother must have taken one look at me and then promptly left me on the priest's doorstep. She was a prostitute I believe, although I never knew her. The priest gave me to an old woman who was the cook in a nearby inn. She had never had a child and she looked after me and loved me until I was five. Then she died.

'After that I survived on the streets of Bari, helped occasionally by other street people who looked out for me and taught me to do tricks and tumbling. When I was fifteen I was spotted by a duke from the north who found me amusing. He took me into his household and it was there that Gesualdo saw me when he came visiting. He bought me from the duke and I've been here in this accursed place ever since. Now I can only hope that he will give me a pension and a place to lay my head when I leave his service.'

'But do you entertain him, Enrico? I asked. 'You know he never smiles, never laughs.' Carnero shrugged his misshapen shoulders.

'Mostly, I listen to him when he talks and I listen to him when he plays. That seems to satisfy him. He asked me for my opinion of the *Canzone Francese di Principe*, The Prince's French Song, the other day.'

'That noise! It sounds like a spider wandering over the keys. What did you say?'

'I said it was an excellent example of Mannerist chromaticism.'

'What on earth does that mean?' Carnero laughed so hard his narrow, sunken chest almost disappeared. 'I haven't the faintest idea. It was something I overheard Ettore Gesualdo say.' I smiled and punched his arm. 'What did our lord and master say to that?'

'He laughed, Laura. He actually laughed. Then he frowned and complained that he suffered from the agonies of the creative spirit

54

"O Death Come Close Mine Eyes"

The last chapter of our long drawn out story, Gesualdo's and mine, took place in the dog days of summer 1613. I was once more alone in the kitchen when Donna Polissena's German assistant found me putting mandragora in the prince's tisane. Of course, she knew what I was doing and she rushed out screaming at the top of her voice, alerting the whole household. Despite my pleas that I was only concocting a soothing brew to aid sleep, I was unmasked as a poisoner, although I was never recognized as Laura Scala.

Once or twice I saw a puzzled expression on the prince's face when he glanced at me, but now he threw off his melancholy and declared that I would be handed over to the Bishop's court to be tried as a witch. Until then I would be locked in an empty room in the servants' quarters.

As I crouched by the door of my room that night I was shaking with fear at the fate awaiting me. I knew I would be tortured as Aurelia had been, then thrown into a cell and forgotten. Visions of Venice and my child swam before me in the darkness. Now I would never see her again.

How long can a night last – a few hours or a hundred years? An endless time passed before I heard a key turn in the lock and a familiar voice whispering, 'Where are you?'

It was Carnero. My old friend had heard of my plight down in the village where he now lived on a meagre allowance from the prince. The dwarf knew every nook and passage in the castle.

'When I heard what had happened to you I got the steward drunk in the tavern and removed his keys. Come, Laura, you can hide in the cellar in my house while I return these keys. When the fuss dies down you can leave for Naples.' I took my sack of belongings and crept after him in the darkness more dead than alive, but I had been given the prod I needed to fulfill my vow. If I could not get near to the prince again I would use another method for my revenge,

On the twentieth of August, just after dawn, I crept into the stables and found Gesualdo's favourite horse, Cesare, his coat gleaming white in the darkness of the stall. The animal's eyes glowed a mad red and I narrowly escaped a kicking as I hid myself, waiting for the groom to saddle the beast. The prince and his entourage always left for the hunt soon after first light. Despite his poor health he continued to ride almost daily. I placed a large thistle under the saddle. If the maddened animal threw his master he would be unlikely to survive. His health was too delicate.

I crept away to the village and so I did not see Don Emanuele ride out on his father's horse. The prince was too ill to ride that day and his son had borrowed the animal. Later I heard that the horse had thrown its rider and Don

Emanuele had died from head injuries. I had killed Donna Maria's son. The curse was still following me all the way from my mother's grave in Sicily.

After the funeral of Don Emanuele, the prince retired to his music room in the tower. A bed was placed there and he lived and slept in that room, clutching the precious relics of his other uncle, the sainted Carlo Borromeo. They said he was overcome with grief at the death of his son, although he showed little affection for him when he was alive. This was the prince's style; just as he was overcome with guilt and sorrow after Donna Maria's death but offered her no affection during the marriage.

As for me, I was like the walking dead. I think I would have thrown myself off the nearest tower had not the thought of my daughter prevented me.

Nineteen days passed before I could do what had to be done. I had been forgotten in the chaos following Don Emanuele's death. No searchers came to look for me and the servants had other things to gossip about.

It was said that the prince had swallowed a topaz as a cure for melancholy, to no avail. The beatings from his pages grew more vicious. It was said that he could not move his bowels unless the beatings took place, during which he would smile seraphically. Preparations were being made for his funeral. It would be like killing a blind kitten, I told myself, but the Prince of Venosa was no kitten. Now, indeed, I had nothing to lose and I found the strength to do what I did; *no hope no fear.*

On the nineteenth day, I prepared a potion in Carnero's

kitchen which would be effective within minutes. From my secret supply I took a few grains of belladonna with some poppy seeds crushed well with thornapple and all steeped in boiling water.

I had never forgotten Sister Antony's lessons. The taste of the devil's cherry was disguised with some sweet juice. I knew that belladonna had been given to the prince on previous occasions. Although lethal in large amounts it can be effective against nervous disorders if the correct dose is used. The measure I poured into the cup would certainly have the desired effect. Not even the Pope's kitchen could have produced anything finer.

That evening, September 9, disguised in a cloak and a wide brimmed hat, I sidled into the castle under the noses of the servants who were huddled over their wine in the kitchen. I glanced in and saw the assembled pages there. The prince was not supposed to be left unattended but gold cannot buy loyalty if you are unloved.

The castle was filled with music. The court musicians had redoubled their efforts to sooth their master's troubled mind and body. Music enveloped me as I climbed the stairs and entered the tower room. The setting sun could be seen through the slitted windows filling the room with a fiery glory as red as the flames of hell that would surely claim his soul that night.

I paused inside the door taking in the smell of candle wax and the sharper tang of a full chamber pot in the corner, further evidence of his servants' neglect. When he saw me he made no attempt to raise the alarm. I lifted his upper body from the bed so that I could pour the drink down his throat. He did not resist.

'I am Laura Scala come to avenge my mistress,' I said softly. Before his body went into its final agony he pointed a trembling hand toward a corner of the room.

'See! They have come for me. Keep them away!' I looked up and saw nothing but shadows but I had no doubt they were there. Donna Maria, the Duke and little Don Alessandro were waiting for him.

As I watched the prince die, his body faded away before me and was replaced with the body of Guido Lotti, the peddler. His dead black eyes looked up at me and his mouth opened in a silent cry of agony. I smiled as the vision faded and the corpse of the prince lay on the bed. Now I had laid both of them to rest.

When I crept softly down the stairs the musicians were still playing in the great hall. I heard the strains of a madrigal by another Englishman, Orlando Gibbons, *O Death Come Close Mine Eyes*. The prince always had morbid tastes.

I left the village of Gesualdo forever. Carnero had told me that the prince was dying and I need not blame myself for his death. The drink I had given him only hastened the event by hours, but I knew better. Later I heard that Donna Polissena had given birth to another daughter. The Prince of Venosa's line was at an end. As the servants liked to say, "God pays debts without money." It was said that the prince and his son were buried together in a double lead coffin. They were to be buried in the church of the Gesu Nuova in Naples but Carnero told me he had seen the coffin interred by the monks in the chapel of Santa Maria delle Grazie in Gesualdo. Why would the monks ignore the prince's last wishes? It can only have been the decision of his wife, Donna Leonora. So, she was not above taking a little revenge after all, the pious one.

Before I prepared to return north to Venice in the train of a visiting bishop, I made a last visit to Donna Maria's tomb in San Domenico Maggiore. 'I have avenged you, mistress,' I whispered. 'I have paid my debt.' But my heart still felt heavy and I felt no lightening of my spirit.

I made my way back to Venice to search for my daughter. At the convent, they would only tell me that she had gone away to another country. I resolved to tell my story, to have it written down ready for my daughter. I felt sure that she would return to Venice – and I would wait for her. Perhaps she was already in the city. I was not inclined to believe the nuns. The Church could not be trusted.

One day I set out to look for a scribe and I was directed to the Franciscans at the Frari church.

55

Venice Easter 1614

Testimony of Brother Agostino

I turned to the woman at my side and pointed across the Grand Canal to where the façade of the Palazzo Dario shone, green and azure and terracotta in the sunlight.

'They say it has a sinister reputation despite its beauty.'

'You mean it is haunted?' she replied. 'the whole city is haunted – a place of rotting stonework, broken dreams and slime-encrusted canals.' The woman shuddered and clutched the stone parapet with hands encased in black woollen mittens despite the warm sunshine.

The air was full of springtime promise and the scent of basil and orange blossom wafted from one of the nearby hidden gardens. Cats were singing on their city perches and the dying echo of the Angelus bell drifted across the water from San Giorgio Maggiore, but the woman was oblivious to the life around her. She continued to stare across the canal.

I looked at her curiously. Who was she and why was she

so insistent that I should write her story? What could a worn old peasant woman from the south have to say that was so important? As if she could read my thoughts the woman turned to me, anxiety crinkling the lines on her careworn face. A few gray, springy curls escaped from under the shawl covering her head.

'I have money to pay you, friar.' I waved this aside.

'I ask only for alms and payment for the writing tools. Come with me to the Frari and we can discuss the matter further.'

As we walked together through the narrow, teeming alleyways I thought the woman was right, after all. This was a strumpet city, full of wickedness and decay where whores called out after barefoot friars offering their wares at special rates. Even the great basilica of St Mark's seems ungodly to my Franciscan eyes...overblown and oriental, almost unchristian.

After a few minutes of silence, the woman assured me that she had an important story to tell. 'I have witnessed terrible things...and I have done wicked deeds – for love. I wish my story to be written down for my daughter's sake. She must know everything about me and about her own history.' I was troubled by her words. This woman needed a confessor not a scribe.

'Why have you not told this story to your daughter personally?' She gave me a melancholy smile.

'I never knew my daughter. She was taken from me at birth and I heard nothing more from the convent orphanage. I left Venice almost twenty years ago and only recently I discovered that she is alive, but I do not know where she lives. When I find her I will give her my story.' She tugged at my arm as if to prevent me from escaping from her.

'I have no learning: once, long ago, my husband taught me to write my name and read a little but I need you to write everything down in the correct manner, elegantly.'

We walked on and entered the Frari church. I retrieved my writing materials and we sat in a quiet corner.

'There is one more thing, Brother.' The woman opened the bundle she was carrying and handed me a package covered in cloth. I removed the cloth and stared at the small, leather-bound book in my hands. I opened it, noting the tiny, uniform handwriting.

'What is this? You told me you could not read or write.' She nodded.

'It is the journal of Don Gesualdo, the Prince of Venosa. I took it from his chamber as he lay dying. His version of the events will prove to you that I am telling the truth.'

I took up my pen with a feeling of foreboding and looked into the woman's unblinking gaze. 'Very well, you can begin now.'

56

The Telling

After the long tale unravelled, I laid down my pen. My hand was stiff, my back ached and my spirit shuddered within me. The woman sat motionless, gazing into the gathering gloom of the church. The day was fading. How long had I spent writing this terrible story? I shook the woman's arm and she seemed to awaken from a dream.

'All your sins are mortal, like the painter. Repent before it is too late!' She appeared not to have heard me. She begged me to intercede for her at the convent. 'I am sure they know something and they will tell you. Is she dead or alive? Where is she? I must know the truth.'

I shook her arm again. 'Come to the altar and pray with me; for the good of your soul and the souls of others.' She followed me obediently but as she knelt next to me on the steps she made no effort to pray. Her eyes were fixed on the great painting by Bellini that was the crowning glory of the church. I prayed aloud -

'Secure Gateway to Heaven, guide my mind, Hail Mary, full of grace…'

I looked up and saw that the woman was staring at the painting of the Madonna and Child with four saints. Below the picture of the Virgin were two angels or cherubs with musical instruments, serenading the holy pair. 'Music,' whispered the old woman, 'always music, ecstasy, penance, the symbols of Gesualdo. These things are never far away.'

I moved back to a pew, followed by the old woman. She cast one last look at the jewel-like colours of the canvas. 'Painting, art' she whispered. 'Someone once told me about those things.'

I begged her once more to repent and be absolved. She shook her head.

'I regret many things and I fear my punishment in the next life, but I cannot repent. I do not believe that Gesualdo repented, either. He just feared hell fire.'

57

Found

On the following day, I presented myself at the convent and the young Mother Superior directed me to an elderly nun who had known the Giovanelli girl well.

'Yes,' said Suor Caterina, 'she was a lively little thing, often in trouble but not bad – just high spirited. She earned a place in the choir; her voice was exceptional even by our standards.'

'Do you know what happened to her?' The nun frowned, trying to recall the details.

'Our girls must leave the convent when they reach fifteen. We try to find positions for them and give them a small dowry. Laura Giovanelli, however, did not settle in Venice when she left here. I remember that an English Lord heard her singing in the chapel and offered to take her to England where she would be a musician in attendance on Queen Anne, who suffered from melancholy, I believe. I do not know if she ever returned.' My heart sank a little. I wanted to find this girl for her mother's sake – to offer that blighted soul some peace.

'Surely that was an unusual, even an unwise thing for a young girl to do?' The nun gave a small shrug.

'Our Mother Superior was not happy about it, I assure you. We were all concerned that Laura was going far away to the court of a Protestant monarch, a heretic. However, the English Ambassador in Venice gave his word that Laura would be kept safe on the journey. In view of that we could not stand in her way. It was a splendid opportunity.'

After thanking the sisters, I returned to the Frari and prayed in its echoing aisles for Maria Laura Giovanelli's safety and for the troubled soul of her mother. Now nothing more remained for me but to return to my Tuscan friary in the hill town of Barga, but Laura Scala had other ideas.

'Please try once more, Brother. Someone here must know where my daughter lives.' She was a foolish woman. Did she think to travel abroad, this peasant woman who had given me her last coins for my services?

The fate of the lost young girl with the beautiful voice, rootless, orphaned, knowing nothing of her past, disturbed my mind. Later, after supper at the friary I remembered the nun's mention of the English Ambassador in Venice. It was possible that he might have some information. I would make one last effort on Laura's behalf.

Sir Henry Wotton received me most graciously and said that he knew of Maria Giovanelli, having heard her sing in London. She had returned to Venice and he would endeavour to find where she lodged. When I conveyed this news to her mother the tired lines on her face were illumined with joy. For the first time, she fell to her knees in the Frari church. I left her in peace, breathing the lingering perfume of candle wax and incense in the whispering gloom.

It is Holy Thursday in this great church and the choristers are singing the prince's Responsaria for Five Voices. Their beautiful young voices echo around me. Is the spirit of the composer listening to his music, full of passion, beauty and guilt? Does he hover in the soft flame of the one candle lit upon the altar? Truly, some part of the man's soul must have been beautiful for such notes to flow from him, from that part not stained with blood, cruelty and the oily sheen of lechery. It is as if I am hearing his music for the first time. Holy Mother! Thank God, I did not know what lay before me in my life.

Brother Agostino has found my daughter and soon I shall meet her if God wills it. I pray that she will greet me as her mother even though I am a stranger to her. I long to tell her about her dear father, about my southern homeland, of the soft hills of Campania shaped like a woman's breasts, the Tramontana wind that makes men mad, and about Noto, beautiful Noto.

Always I feel the prince's shadow near me. Has he found liberation from his nightmares…in what ghastly shades does his soul wander, can he hear the music of the spheres or the lingering rise and fall of his Responsaria?

The candle is out now and one voice soars in the darkness, "O vos omnes…all ye that pass by, behold and see if there be any sorrow like unto my sorrow."

Four days later I was leaning over the Rialto Bridge watching the constant flow of gondolas and other ships.

Behind me, In the Rialto market, the cries of the fish vendors mingled with the shrill voices of housewives disputing the prices.

Lost in contemplation, I closed my eyes, remembering Laura's description of the death of her husband, seeing in my mind the gunpowder boat approaching the gondola, the flames shooting skywards and the loud explosion.

I shuddered as the sound seemed to ring in my ears, then I realized that someone was calling my name. Opening my eyes, I looked down as a gondola stopped under the bridge and an elegant figure in green velvet stood up and waved at me.

'Brother Agostino, come down here.' It was the English Ambassador inviting me into his private gondola. Feeling a little foolish, I clutched my tattered brown robe about me and hurried down the steps to the boat. Two of the ambassador's bodyguards helped me into the swaying vessel where Sir Henry placed a hand on my shoulder and greeted me affably.

'Forgive the sudden greeting, Brother. I recognized you as we swept along. I have some news for you.' We sat together and the English representative to the Serene Republic chatted amicably in a manner that contrasted sharply with the attitudes of the local nobility.

'I think I have found your lost singer, my friend. I have been told that she lodges in a house at the corner of the Campiello de Ca'Barbaro in the Zattere district. It is not far to go. We will take you to the nearest point on the Grand Canal.'

Once again, I could only stammer my thanks as I received another friendly wave from Sir Henry. I made my way towards the rear of the Palazzo Dario, the building that always gave me a slight frisson of fear.

I made enquiries of a young water seller who set down her yoke and water pots and gestured at a tall, narrow house behind an acacia tree.

'She lodges there, in the house of the German woman.'

I stood outside the house for a moment overcome with emotion now that I was about to solve the last piece of Laura's puzzle. My hand went to my breast where I had placed the pouch containing the papers. When I knocked at the door a small girl opened it and regarded me insolently.

'We want no beggars here, not even holy ones; it is my mistress's orders.' I pushed the door open with one hand and held the girl at arm's length. She could not have been more than ten years old.

'I am here to see the Signorina Giovanelli on important business. Kindly take me to her at once.' An elderly woman dressed in the German fashion appeared from a back room and surveyed me calmly.

'The signorina is with a pupil. You may wait here if you wish. She will be finished soon.'

I sat on a bench in the gloomy hall for a further fifteen minutes before being shown upstairs to a room overlooking the canal. A young boy carrying a lute slipped past me and finally I was alone with Laura's daughter.

The young woman was facing the window. As she turned to face me I held my breath. Maria Laura Giovanelli was beautiful: tall, slender, with the slim, long-fingered hands of a musician. Her face was a perfect oval with dark eyes and she had her mother's mass of curly hair tied up in a velvet ribbon. She wore a gown of pomegranate red silk trimmed with black velvet, with lace ruffles at her neck and wrists. Her regard was serious and steady. I bowed before her.

'I do not believe I know you, Brother, but Sir Henry told me you were anxious to find me.' She gave a sudden, happy smile. 'What can I do for you? I do not think you plan to take singing lessons.' I drew the papers from my breast and held them out to her.

'I have come to give you these, signorina. I have come to tell you who you are and where you come from.' The young woman arched her delicate, dark brows.

'I know where I come from, Brother. I am a citizen of Venice. I was born here and my grandmother placed me in the orphanage after the death of my father. I know nothing of my mother. They were poor people, I believe. The nuns gave that information to me. I also know that my grandmother died soon after I was taken in. She drowned in the Grand Canal.'

She gestured to a seat by the window and we sat together silently while she gazed out of the window once more. I noted the resemblance to her mother, a more beautiful version of Laura Scala – and a far more accomplished one. I felt my face grow hot when she turned her head and caught me staring at her.

'I have a suspicion that your story will not be one I would wish to hear. Why are you troubling me with this? I am twenty years old and I accepted long ago that I am an orphan, without family. Fortunately, my grandmother ensured that I would be educated and trained as a musician.

'Music is my life, my passion and my substitute family. It has enabled me to travel and to provide for myself. I have enjoyed the patronage of royalty, Brother. Why do I need to hear sad stories from the past?' I rustled the papers, troubled by her remarks.

'I have come to tell you the truth, signorina, so that you will no longer live a lie. Your mother did not die. She is not lost. She is here in Venice and she asked my help in finding you.'

Maria Laura Giovanelli's cheeks turned pale and she leaned on her chair for support for several moments. I noticed a small carafe of wine on a table and poured some for her. She did not speak for some time. Then she turned to me.

'When I was a child growing up in the orphanage I used to pray that my mother would come for me. We all did that, all the children in that place. We day-dreamed that our parents were princes and princesses who had suffered misfortunes, but who would claim us eventually and take us into a new life of riches. Most of all we wanted to reassure ourselves that someone loved us. When my mother did not come it was assumed by the nuns that she had died. I gave up hope and trained myself not to think about her.' A single tear rolled down her cheek.

I was at a loss. I have no experience of dealing with female tears. Gently, I placed the papers in her hands and urged her to read them.

'Send a message to me when you have read them. There will be many questions you will want to ask.' As I left the room I said, 'Your mother will be very proud when she hears of your success.'

Several days passed before I received a message directing me to meet her on the Fondamenta not far from where the Giovanelii family lodged many years ago. The Easter celebrations had passed.

I found her wrapped in a long grey cloak at the entrance to what Venetians call a sottoportego, an alley leading to the water's edge. Fresh flowers adorned a tiny shrine to the Virgin set in the wall.

When I drew near I could see that the young woman's eyes were red-rimmed as if she had been crying and her cheeks were pale. I took her hand and patted it, not knowing what else to do. She managed a shadow of a smile.

'So, Brother, it was as I expected, a long and sorry tale.' I nodded and patted her hand again. Slowly she began to speak and I attempted to answer her questions. 'No, I had never met the Prince of Venosa, thank God. He died before your mother told me her story.'

'You mean after my mother murdered him?' she said quietly.

'Yes, she should not have taken vengeance in that manner but her sins were committed out of love and loyalty. That must count in her favour.'

'And what of my grandmother? I always thought well of her for giving me to the nuns.'

'She was an evil woman, but good can come from evil

sometimes. The ways of the Almighty are mysterious.' The young woman stared into the canal where the oily waters bubbled a little as if a large fish was swimming by.

'Gesualdo, The Prince of Venosa' she said thoughtfully. 'I know his music. I have sung it many times. Everything comes from him, doesn't it? I would not exist if he had not done what he did. And what of the artist, Caravaggio? His name is renowned throughout Europe.' I nodded agreement.

'I have seen some of his paintings in Rome. He was a terrible blasphemer but God marked him with greatness.'

'And my mother loved him,' she said softly.

'She loves you, my child. A mother's love never dies.' I gestured to where a woman stood very still, a few yards away. Signorina Giovanelli turned towards her mother as I slipped away. When I looked back I saw two curly heads close together, one grey and one black. Flower petals were falling from the little shrine and a faint scent of lavender drifted on the air.

Epilogue

Laura Scala and her daughter left for the New World in June 1614 using Donna Maria's last pearl to pay their passage. In Mexico City Maria Laura was engaged as music teacher to the daughter of the Viceroy.

Laura Scala died suddenly in the church of San Juan Bautista in Coyoacan on the anniversary of Gesualdo's death in 1617.

A Note on Gesualdo's Music

Mannerism was fashionable between the late Renaissance and the Baroque period, (1530-1630 approx). Gesualdo was a follower of this style and the madrigal was the favoured mannerist form, "Fanciful and anxious in spirit, superficial and tortured in style, its keynote is ambivalence."

The sighs and melancholy passions of unrequited love were keynotes of Gesualdo's madrigals and were later transformed into the religious agony of music for the church, full of guilt and desperation.

Gesualdo frequently composed to a set text such as the poems of Tasso. Of the six books of madrigals known to have existed, books one and two are still performed regularly. They were usually written for five voices, sometimes for six or seven.

The Responsaria for Holy Week, published in 1611, remains Gesualdo's most celebrated work. Written as part of the liturgy for Holy Thursday it is "full of daring harmonies and strange, imaginative, chromatic experiments" that would not be heard again until the modern era.

Although praised in his own century, Gesualdo's work fell out of favour in the 18th century and was largely forgotten or ignored. He was regarded as "the crank of chromaticism." His name was kept alive largely through his notorious private life, the subject of books, plays, an opera, a musical, a ballet by the New York City Ballet, and more recently, a film by Werner Herzog – *Death for Five Voices.*

The Russian composer, Igor Stravinsky was an enthusiast for Gesualdo's work and was largely responsible for restoring the prince's musical reputation. He made a visit to the castle of Gesualdo in 1956 finding it semi-derelict and occupied by squatters. The castle also suffered further destruction in an earthquake in the 1960s. More recently it provided a memorable backdrop to the Werner Herzog film.

Even in his own lifetime, opinion on his musical achievements was divided. A contemporary, Alfonso Fontarelli wrote, "It is obvious that his art is infinite, but it is full of attitudes and moves in an extraordinary way. However, everything is a matter of taste…"

Gesualdo occupies a unique position in the history of Western music – a prince who achieved fame as a composer. In his own time, it was considered an eccentric and ungentlemanly occupation.

The prince's music continues to grow in popularity. The Gesualdo Consort of London, the Tallis Scholars and several other early music groups are bringing his work to modern audiences. The Gesualdo Conservatory of Music is based in Venosa and the Fondazione Carlo Gesualdo in Avellino is the international centre for study and research into the prince's music.

- I am indebted to the work of Professor Glen Watkins for information on the life and music of Gesualdo.
- Gesualdo: The Man and His Music. 1992
- The Gesualdo Hex. 2010

Author's Note

I have followed historical facts and dates as far as possible. Laura Scala existed. She was described as the maidservant of Donna Maria d'Avalos, Gesualdo's wife.

She was called as a witness by the Viceroy's court after the murders, but she had disappeared. I have given her a story.

There is no record of the artist Caravaggio meeting Gesualdo or painting a 'musical' portrait for him, but he was in Naples at the right time. There are several lost paintings by Caravaggio and I have imagined one of them.

Quotations:

"Many waters cannot quench love" -Song of Solomon

"O Death Come Close Mine Eyes"- Orlando Gibbons

Lightning Source UK Ltd.
Milton Keynes UK
UKHW03f1517060418
320640UK00001B/6/P